THE ENGLISH CAPTAIN

The English Captain introduces Captain Jethro Cockerill Penhaligon—"Cocky" Penhaligon to his friends a new and welcome figure in naval fiction.

The year is 1800, two years after Nelson's victory at the Nile, and British shipping in the Mediterranean is being harassed by *Gironde 74*, one of the few French survivors.

Penhaligon is summoned to the Capodimonte Palace, where, expecting an admonishment from the "little Admiral" for a duel in which one of the leading ministers in Naples has been killed, he is told instead that he is to be promoted to *Avenger*, a 34-gun frigate: his task to take, burn or destroy the French ship of the line.

How Penhaligon tackles this daunting task while still enjoying the amatory adventures for which he has become notorious makes enthralling reading.

The details of naval action and day-to-day life in a fighting ship of the time are authentic, and the sea battles measure up to some of the best in naval fiction.

You will be hearing more of Penhaligon.

The English Captain

by

SIMON WHITE

ST. MARTIN'S PRESS
New York

ROBERT HALE LIMITED
London

© Simon White 1977
First published in the United States of America 1977

St. Martin's Press, Inc.
175 Fifth Avenue
New York, N.Y. 10010

Library of Congress Card Number 77-3191

Library of Congress Cataloging in Publication Data
White, Simon.
    The English Captain.
I. Title.
PZ4.W58852 En 3 [PR6073. H525]
823′.9′14 77-3191
ISBN 0-312-25357-5

First published in Great Britain 1977

ISBN 0 7091 5944 7

Robert Hale Limited
Clerkenwell House
Clerkenwell Green
London EC1R 0HT

Printed and bound in Great Britain by A. Wheaton & Co., Exeter

ONE

WHEN Francesco Domenico Alberto Giovanni Sannazzaro, Duke of Potenza, Minister of State to the newly emancipated Bourbon king, returned unexpectedly to his palace in the Via di Toledo and discovered, on the tearful admission of a maid, that his wife was in bed with a foreign gentleman, he left a note, politely worded, begging her to meet him in his study on the following morning, and straight away, after cuffing the maid with sufficient severity to knock out several teeth, returned to his mistress in the Via Calva. The foreign gentleman, Captain Jethro Cockerill Penhaligon, a naval officer of some renown—or notoriety, according to whichever faction, British or French, Dutch and Spanish, you supported—duly apprised, returned to his ship, the tiny sloop of war *Mallorca*, then at anchor in Naples Bay, and awaited developments.

They arrived at seven bells in the forenoon watch in the person of an elegant gentleman, powdered and bewigged after the manner of the times, and wearing shoes with silver buckles, silk stockings, superbly cut breeches and jacket of bottle-green with a sateen waistcoat to match, and a cravat which flowed like a well-conducted waterfall from his neck to the deep V of his lapels.

This gentleman, who introduced himself as the Marquis of something or other—his English was poor and his voice indistinct since he felt it necessary to cover his nose with a wisp of handkerchief against the smells of a ship of war—informed Penhaligon that the Duke of Potenza was demanding satisfaction, that he, the Marquis of something or other, had the honour to be his second, and if the English captain had any preferences for place, time or weapons the Duke would be happy to give them consideration. Penhaligon, who was expecting orders to sail at any time, suggested the open ground before the Castello Sant' Elmo at dawn five days hence, and, since he expressed no preference for weapons, pistols at twenty paces were chosen. He had not forgotten, nor was he unduly disturbed, since he was reckoning to be at sea within five days, by the thought that the Duke was not only head of the state police but the most formidable duellist in Naples.

It was only later, when he learnt that at the meeting so courteously arranged the Duke had taken a horse whip to his wife and beaten her into a state of insensibility, that Penhaligon changed his mind and avoided the Capodimonte Palace and the home of Sir William Hamilton, the ambassador, where Nelson, who was still recovering from the wounds received more than a year ago at the Nile, might see him and remember that *Mallorca* was still in port.

He also took to practising for several hours a day with a pistol, using as target a square of wood the size of a man's head, fixed to the taffrail. The ambassador and the English-born Prime Minister, Acton, came aboard and urged him to swallow his pride and accept whatever humiliations the Duke might demand. Nelson, when he thought of the matter at all, tried to decide whom he should promote as captain of *Mallorca*.

In fact, the decision was unnecessary. At dawn on the morning of the fifth day Penhaligon met the wife-beater, murderer, chief of police and scion of Neapolitan society at a distance of twenty paces and, with the coolness and precision which had marked all his actions at sea, shot him dead.

Within minutes, leaving the marquis and his friends to mourn the departed, he returned with his second to the carriage below, where his steward, a short, barrel-chested Irishman named Baghot, was rubbing eyes and nose and swearing heartfelt oaths of relief as he laid out a tray of cold chicken and ham to be washed down with a bottle of Marsala, and sat down to eat.

Penhaligon breakfasted slowly, in silence and with no small sense of relief, for, despite his casual appearance, he knew that it had been a close-run thing.

It was a warm, dry morning, the town of Naples, beautiful at this distance, and the blue curve of the bay lay below him; in the distance Vesuvius belched smoke and flames as it woke to a new day. Skylarks were in the heavens, there was a scent of thyme and lemon blossom on the air; somewhere along the hill a girl was singing.

It was still early morning when he reached Via di Toledo, and he guessed from the surprise and pleasure on the faces of ostler and footman as he alighted at the door that the result of the duel was still unknown. So much the better. The butler who met him at the entrance and the maid, weeping and smiling as she knelt to kiss his hand, followed him across the hall, but then stood, as though too overcome for words, as he climbed the stairs.

Maddalena's door was locked. He rapped once, twice, and waited, affecting not to hear the tremulous "Who is it?" He heard the key turning, the door opened an inch or two, he caught the fragrance of her hair.

"Cocky! Darling!" He held her in his arms with the door still open as she shed the worst of her tears. Then with his arm round her shoulders he led her inside.

It was noon or thereabouts when a timid knock and the voice of the maid, still sibilant from the loss of teeth, broke their idyll. Maddalena, moving stiffly from the bed and quickly covering herself with a robe, went to the door.

"If you please, my lady—"

The note was for Captain Penhaligon, His Majesty's sloop of war *Mallorca*: "You are hereby directed and required to report to me at the Capodimonte Palace at noon today", and was signed, "Nelson of Bronte".

"What time is it?"

9

"If you please, sir," the maid said, ducking a curtsy without taking her eyes from her naked hero on the bed, "it's ten minutes after noon."

"The devil take it! Don't they know I'm busy?" He smiled and rolled on to his side as Maddalena, after shutting the door, came and sat beside him.

"Who wants you?"

"The admiral."

She sighed and, without any obvious attempt at coquetry, took his hand and pressed it against her breast. "You'll have to go."

"I suppose so."

"Will there be trouble?"

He shrugged as he caressed her gently, feeling the softness of her skin. "Who knows? If there is, there's no point in meeting it half-way. I'll go when I'm ready."

"But you said—"

He put his hands on her shoulders and drew her towards him, smothering her half-hearted protests with kisses. The robe slipped from her body and, being of the best Moorish silk, slid voluptuously from bed to floor.

They made love hungrily, without care or inhibition, as though happiness, which had previously eluded them through fear of her husband, was suddenly theirs. Sometimes in her passion she cried out, but whether from emotion or from the pain of her cruelly lacerated shoulders he could not tell.

When it was over they lay side by side, fingers interlocked, listening to the garden noises, the twitter of birds, the rasp of cicadas and the song of a maid at the washtub, a serving girl, Maddalena said, not long from the country, who was still young enough and sufficiently inexperienced to find city life enchanting. Outside, shading the garden and the ornamental ponds, was a willow, whose branches, moving like tresses in the breeze, hid, or partially hid, the smiling face of spring beyond.

"I must go." He stood up and leant, still naked, at the open

10

window. A dog, dazed by the heat, half raised its head and then, too tired to bark, lay back again. The maid at the wash-tub was still singing.

Maddalena watched him as he dressed, breeches, stockings, shoes, shirt with darns lovingly worked by some feminine hand, waistcoat, kerchief, jacket, and it was only when he buckled on his sword and took up his hat that she swung herself from the bed and ran to hold him. "Cocky, don't go!"

"I must." He disengaged himself gently, mindful, now that love was satisfied, of the admiral's message and curious to learn the reason for his summons.

"I'll be back."

She watched him tearfully through the half-open doorway as he descended the stairs, and it was only after he had passed from view that she turned and threw herself on the bed.

"Sir!" The girl, Maddalena's maid, came hurrying towards him. "Let me call your carriage."

He smiled. "Don't worry. If my steward isn't indoors he'll be at the stables." He caught her look of embarrassment as she tried to cover her teeth, and added, "I'm surprised he's not with you. It's not often he can resist a pretty girl."

Her face lit up with surprise and pleasure, and before she could put her hand to her mouth he had leant forward and kissed her on the lips. "No more than I can."

Outside, heat was shimmering above the courtyard. The dog he had seen from the bedroom window thumped its tail but still made no attempt to rise.

"Where to, sir?" Baghot, who had been waiting this last hour in the elusive shade of an orange tree, spoke gruffly, in a tone Penhaligon knew well, as he rolled across the courtyard to open the carriage door.

"Capodimonte."

"To see the admiral, then?" the steward probed, while Penhaligon climbed carefully into the ancient carriage, and then, his red face appearing again like a half-moon at the open window, "We'll be getting orders?"

11

"Perhaps."

The road to Capodimonte, known as the Via di Roma, ran straight, with scarcely a bend, from the fashionable quarter round Castel Nuovo, through an agglomeration of shops and taverns and dwelling-houses, some well-to-do, others poor and ramshackle beyond belief, until, beyond the Via Foria, it emerged joyfully into a countryside rich with olive groves and orchards heavy with blossom and graced by a few fine houses and farmsteads. The palace lay at the end of an avenue of trees.

"Halt!" A palace guard, sweating in scarlet jacket with cross-belt and pouches, boots, skin-tight trousers and shako, barred their passage. "State your business."

Directed by Baghot, who spoke no language but English and that indifferently, the guard came to the open window and saluted.

"Penhaligon of *Mallorca* to see the admiral."

"Yes, sir." Standing stiffly to attention, the guard nodded him forward.

He had never been to the palace before, and now, recalling the events of the morning, was less than confident of the reception he would receive. The Duke had been the King's friend, a minister of state : it was possible that he would be arrested.

He climbed the steps and, returning the salute of another sentry at the door, he saw in the dim light of the reception hall a figure clad, as it seemed, in some diaphanous material that ill-concealed the shape or grace of her body.

"Cocky! I thought you were never coming."

"Emma." He took her hands and, since no one was looking, soundly kissed her. "I am more than relieved to see you."

"Relieved?" She pouted. "Is that the best you can do?" She waited, but only for a moment. "Never mind. You are late, very late. Didn't you know that *he* is waiting?" She shook her head. "As though you were not in enough trouble already!"

"That's what I thought." He grinned. "If I'm to be hanged, at least I've had time to collect my thoughts, another hour of freedom."

"With that woman?" She was watching him intently; he realised that as he met her bright, demanding stare with a look so guileless that any woman but Emma Hamilton might have been deluded. "Come!" she ordered. "Admit it. You've been with the Sannazzaro woman?"

"The Duchessa?" He frowned and managed a stern expression, realising from experience that a word out of place at this moment could set her off on one of her fish-wife tantrums. "I've seen her, yes—to express my condolences. You heard that she has lost her husband?"

"I heard!" She scowled, half-way between amusement and anger. Then, to his great relief, she burst out laughing. "Condolences, my crotch! A good roll on the bed more likely, and with her still sore from her master's beating. Come!" She pushed her finger into his ribs. "Admit it. You've been with her." She shook her head in reluctant admiration. "You certainly waste no time."

He shrugged. "Life is short: you know my philosophy. Besides, there are more ways than one of comforting a woman."

"Only one that you know."

"Well, I'm here: a bit late, perhaps, but my conscience is clear."

"Conscience? What do you know about that?"

"Enough to realise that I've offended the most beautiful woman in Naples—for which there is no excuse."

She moued prettily and was instantly serious. "Come. There's no time to talk. Horatio is anxious to see you. He's very angry."

"And Sir William?"

She grimaced. "My husband is with him."

"So—it doesn't look good."

"It will look worse if you keep them waiting any longer."

She turned, but before she could move across the hall he caught her arm. "No. Wait!" She looked at him enquiringly. "They've been at it an hour or more: it's all decided. Whether I'm to be court-martialled, sent home or thrown into jail: they know what they are going to do."

"So?"

He smiled down at her and stroked her arm. "It occurs to me that since my time is short, or likely to be so, it is stupid, no, worse than stupid, to be standing here talking when across there is an ante-room with a lock on the door and a couch."

For a moment, he knew, she was tempted. Her face, which was pert rather than beautiful, looked up at his with an expression that was soft and tender and carried, in her eyes rather than in any movement of her perfectly formed lips, a hint of the passion which, although now dormant, could so easily be aroused. She sighed and made no attempt to repel him as his arms enclosed her and one hand moved beneath the shoulder of her dress. Her lips were soft, her body yielding— but only for a moment.

With an impatient gesture she pushed him away. "For God's sake, Cocky! Is that all you can think of?"

"While you are around, yes."

She pretended to be angry, but he knew that it was more for her sake than for his. "I'll tell them you are here."

"If you must." He put on a look of concern, which was not all play-acting, and with his hat correctly held in the crook of his arm and his sword at his side he drew himself up to his full six feet three and saluted. "To the scaffold, then."

She smiled and patted his arm. "It's not come to that yet, thank God! I'll see what I can do."

"Thank you." He watched her as she crossed the hall, and then called after her. "Emma!"

"Yes?"

"Thank you."

The rooms which Nelson used were in the west wing, once the banqueting halls, with tessellated floors and ornate ceilings and paintings by Caravaggio, Domenicho and other lesser-known artists on the walls. Penhaligon sat on a brocaded chair in the ante-room and waited.

Twenty minutes passed before Emma Hamilton reappeared. She looked angry but triumphant, cheeks flushed, eyes bright, and a determined set to her jaw.

"The admiral will see you now."

Nelson was a slight man of less than medium height and he appeared dwarfed by the huge stall, more throne than chair, on which he sat. His face was pale and emaciated, his right sleeve, pinned to his jacket, and his one good eye—his left—which watched unblinkingly as Penhaligon crossed the room, far from detracting from his appearance rather endowed it with strength and dignity. Penhaligon, who suddenly felt less sure of himself, acknowledged this : Rear-Admiral Lord Nelson, Duke of Bronte, was, on closer acquaintance, a formidable character.

"You are late."

"Yes, my lord : my apologies."

They waited, Nelson with expression grim and forbidding, Sir William fidgeting, Penhaligon, still clasping hat and sword, apparently, albeit falsely, at ease.

"Am I to be denied an excuse, then, some explanation?"

"Beg pardon, my lord : I was delayed."

"By what? You received my orders?"

"Yes, my lord. There were—private matters."

"God bless my soul!" It was Sir William Hamilton who uttered the exclamation. Nelson remained quite still, lips firm, the single, all-seeing eye appraising.

"The Duke of Potenza, my lord, was killed this morning. It was my unhappy duty to apprise the Duchess of her loss."

"And this took—how long?"

"An hour, my lord, possibly more. She was very upset."

"Indeed!"

"In fact, so upset that it seemed nothing less than my Christian duty to stay and comfort her." Penhaligon coughed.

"It was, my lord, or so I thought, what would be expected of any British officer and gentleman."

Nelson's expression did not alter, the inquisitorial stare remained unwavering. "I see."

There was an embarrassing silence during which Penhaligon, who was still standing to attention, braced himself to withstand the admiral's scrutiny, guessing that Nelson was using this tack to breach his defences. In fact, it was Emma's husband, the elderly, good-natured ambassador, who broke.

"Good God, Penhaligon! You have killed the duke, a senior minister. Don't you realise what you have done?"

"It was a quarrel, sir, not of my making, a duel fairly fought."

"Fairly fought!" Sir William exclaimed. "Do you suppose the King is going to accept that as an excuse when he hears?"

"So he has not been told?"

Sir William hesitated and glanced towards the admiral. "Not yet."

"The truth is, Penhaligon," Nelson said, "we don't know what consequences your action will have. The Duke of Potenza was a friend of the King." He hesitated and then, unexpectedly and rather charmingly, smiled. "But not of mine."

"You mean, my lord, that the King may want my neck?"

"Perhaps. I hope it won't come to that. More importantly, it may, it could, affect our whole alliance with the kingdom of the Two Sicilies." For the first time Nelson relaxed and with a gesture of the hand invited Penhaligon to take a chair. "Our position is strong, of course, you might think impregnable since the kingdom is only sustained by the power of the British Navy, but the King is a proud man—all the Bourbons are proud and stiff-necked. If he considers that he has been insulted, his feelings flouted, he might be persuaded to listen to the blandishments of Napoleon's agents who are here in Naples despite my protests."

"But, my lord, any alliance with the French could mean only one thing: servitude."

The admiral nodded. "One must hope that the King will see it that way."

Penhaligon said, "I am sorry, my lord, that my duel has caused you embarrassment."

Nelson accepted the apology with an inclination of the head and, after a momentary hesitation, leant across and rang a bell. "You will take a glass of claret with me?"

"I would be honoured, my lord."

The wine, brought on a silver tray by an extravagantly caparisoned flunkey, was the final seal of forgiveness. Nelson raised his glass. "Your health, Penhaligon, and let me say that whatever your peccadilloes ashore, your record shows that you are a good sailor."

"My lord!" Penhaligon felt himself blushing. "Coming from you, that is praise indeed."

"It is praise well earned. We have noted with pleasure your exploits off the Spanish coast. To inflict such confusion among enemy shipping, especially with such a small, ill-considered craft, calls for the highest standards of seamanship and resolution."

Unusually embarrassed, Penhaligon took a quaff of claret and, so great was his confusion, began to choke.

"And ye've not done badly by prize money?" Sir William suggested, his face beaming, and Penhaligon realised for the first time that Emma's husband was a kindly man, who worshipped Nelson and, now that the admiral had signified approval, was genuinely happy to follow suit.

"Not badly at all, sir, and I'm grateful, although to be honest I'd be happier if our action had been against a more worthy foe."

The sudden silence surprised him. He was conscious of their exchanged glances, and Sir William, a trifle too heartily, asked, "You know they have a name for you, the French and Spanish? They call you simply The English Captain."

Penhaligon shrugged. "At least it's accurate, sir. I wonder what they would call me if I took one of their ships of war."

"You've done that already," Nelson pointed out. "*Volante* and *Aristide*. I tell you without flattery that we consider those encounters to have been models of single-ship action."

"A brig, my lord, and badly handled frigate. They may look good on paper, but what I want, what every English captain wants, is to engage a ship of the line."

"What a fire-eater!" Sir William laughed, and again Penhaligon felt that they were holding back.

Nelson had pushed away his wine and was sitting far back in his chair—ready for action? The ambassador was looking at his hands.

"The truth is, Penhaligon—" Nelson began, and then stopped with a gesture of annoyance as someone knocked at the door. "Yes?"

"Your pardon, my lord." An equerry came across to the table with a note. "I understand it is urgent, my lord—from the Prime Minister."

"Very well."

Nelson waited for the man to leave before opening the single sheet, and then only glanced at it before passing it over to the ambassador.

"Acton came to see me this morning," Nelson explained, "since he was as concerned as we are about the repercussions following your duel. His feeling, with which Sir William and I concurred, was that we should delay news of the Duke's death as long as possible. Fortunately, the King is away on a hunting trip. This note," he motioned towards the paper in Sir William's hand, "tells us that unfortunately the King has heard the news—how we don't know, although my guess is from one of Napoleon's agents—and is expected back in Naples tomorrow."

"Which leaves us a day," Sir William observed, "less than a day."

Nelson nodded. "To get you out of the country, Penhaligon:

18

that's what we decided. Whatever demands the King may make, and I repeat that he is likely to be very angry, our position, Sir William's and mine, will be easier if the culprit has left Naples."

"That is no problem, my lord," Penhaligon said. "*Mallorca* is ready: food, water, powder and shot: we can sail on an hour's notice."

"Good, for that's all you are likely to get. The sooner you put Naples behind you the better, for it occurs to me that although the King is not expected until tomorrow he could quite easily send a message by fast rider ordering your arrest, a message I would be hard put to refuse."

"I'll leave at once," Penhaligon said. "We can clear the bay by dusk." He stopped. "If I could have your orders, my lord."

"What? Oh, yes." Nelson's expression went blank and he remained quite still, eyes closed and chin sunk upon his breast. A newcomer to the room could have been forgiven for thinking that he was asleep, but Penhaligon had the feeling that everything in the room, he, Sir William, whose expression seemed unaccountably strained, the decanter and glasses on the table, the Caravaggio and the two Domenichos on the walls, the desk and the carved ceiling and the elegant mosaic on the floor were leagues from the admiral's thoughts at that moment. He was weighing a decision.

"Your orders?" He returned with difficulty to the present, like a man wakened from sleep. His eye saw, yet failed to see, Sir William and the larger of the Domenichos behind him, and it was not until his gaze settled on Penhaligon that he came to life.

"Your orders, captain, are to sail as you are ready, but in any case not later than an hour before sunset."

"I can sail immediately, my lord, as soon as I return to my ship. Give me an hour to collect the watch on shore."

"You will set course for Minorca," Nelson continued, as though he had not heard, "passing south of Sardinia."

He waited as though expecting an objection, but Penhaligon remained silent. If the admiral wanted him to avoid the quickest route, between Corsica and Sardinia, he must have his reasons.

"At Minorca you will take on fresh water and stores, sufficient for a long stay at sea," Nelson continued. (Penhaligon's hopes rose, a mission to the West Indies, perhaps, or even India.) "You will then until further notice operate off the Spanish coast as you have done so successfully before."

"Disrupting coastal traffic," Penhaligon asked, "taking or sinking any merchant ships I find, intercepting any Spanish ships of war?"

"Something like that. I'll send you written orders."

"Very good, my lord." He felt vaguely disappointed, he couldn't say why, since this was exactly what *Mallorca* had been doing so successfully—and profitably for all on board, officers and crew—these last few months.

"And these are all your orders, my lord?" Sir William asked. He, too, for some reason, seemed disappointed.

Nelson gave one of his rare smiles. "Not quite. Harassing the coastal traffic is important, make no mistake. The Spanish, who are only fighting at Napoleon's insistence, won't take kindly to the destruction of their shipping." He picked up his empty glass and twirled it by the stem. "Your real object, Penhaligon, is even more important—to seek, take, burn, sink or destroy a French ship of the line. You are going out after *Gironde*."

If Penhaligon was surprised he had far too much control to show it. *Gironde*, a 74-gun ship of the line, had been a thorn in the flesh of the British for too long: every Englishman knew that. One of the few French ships to escape the holocaust of the Nile, she had sailed westwards, badly holed and under jury rig, more than a year ago and by a combination of luck and good seamanship had reached the allied port of Barcelona. From there, after a time for repairs and refitting, she had emerged when wind and naval intelligence

20

were propitious to plunder British ships of war unfortunate to meet her single-handed. *Mayflower*, sloop of war, *Devon Rose*, bombard, and the frigate *Xerxes* had fallen. Before leaving for the blockade of Brest, Admiral Lord Keith, the Command-in-Chief, had sent a ship of the line, *Norfolk 74*, with escorting frigates to intercept her, but after six months of alarms and excursions in which French and Spanish intelligence appeared uncannily superior to our own, Nelson, in Keith's absence, had withdrawn them. Now he was sending *Mallorca*.

It was scarcely credible. *Gironde* was a first-rater, with enough weight of metal to blow *Mallorca* out of the water at the first broadside. The odds were ludicrous. *Mallorca*, a mere 170 tons, armed with sixteen four-pounders, was a cockleshell of a ship, however skilfully he might sail her. It was like pitting a company of foot against the Grande Armée.

Yet, whatever reservations Penhaligon felt, and they were many, for his judgment of sea warfare was exceptional, he could not restrain a feeling of pride that the Navy in its arrogance could feel such a confrontation reasonable. It was true that whatever successes Napoleon might have had on land, and these, although impressive, had generally been against indifferent, ill organised, although frequently numerically superior, opposition, on sea the British Navy ruled supreme. The Navy believed, and often proved, that one British Jack was worth six or seven Frogs. West Indies, Lorient, Cape St Vincent, the glorious first of June : the English won, and won handsomely, whenever they managed to lure a reluctant enemy to sea. But the ultimate proof, which Nelson himself had supplied, had been the Nile, one of the most complete and devastating victories in naval history. These were proud times.

"You understand your orders?"

"Yes, my lord."

"And you have no—doubts?"

Penhaligon's face was expressionless. "Doubts, my lord?"

"That *Mallorca*, a sloop of war, should be taking on the pride of the French navy?" Sir William suggested. He was a good fellow and could not bear to see Penhaligon kept in suspense any longer.

"Sir William means," Nelson said, "that an opportunity has arisen, as happens only too frequently in times of war. Henry Chisholm of *Avenger*, who was badly wounded at St Vincent, is coming ashore. I am attaching him to my staff." He smiled, and at that moment Penhaligon realised why officers and men were prepared to fight and follow the little admiral to death.

"You will not be seeking *Gironde* in *Mallorca*," Nelson said. "I am appointing you captain into *Avenger*."

TWO

THAT evening while the sun was still high, although a haze blurred the horizon and shadows were bringing twilight to the streets, *Avenger* put to sea.

There was a shore breeze, too slight to fill the canvas but sufficient to curve the topsails and, as the helmsman spun the wheel, bringing it astern, to give steerage way. Yards were hoisted, sheets hauled home, and with scarcely a sound above the slap of bare feet on the decks, the occasional cries of the boatswain and a faint hiss from the cutwater, *Avenger* glided across the bay.

She was a good ship : Penhaligon felt that as he stood, feet astride, hands clasped behind back, sailor fashion, and watched from his privileged position on the quarterdeck a strange crew under strange officers handling a ship that was so much bigger than *Mallorca*, although still tiny compared with *Gironde* or any other ship of the line, that he felt humbled. His cabin, which in fact was no more than a modest area bulkheaded from the main cabin and that half-filled by one of the eighteen-pounder guns, was so much more spacious than the hen coop he had occupied on *Mallorca* that Baghot, after he had brought his dunnage across in a dinghy, had been impressed. "Holy Mary, sir ! We'll need more furniture."

Strange ship and a strange crew. He thought he understood why Nelson had ordered the longer, safer route to Minorca. Four, five days, or less if the winds were favourable, would be scarce time to get the feel of his ship and, even more important, the measure of officers and men.

"Steady as she goes."

23

That was Lubbock, the master, standing at his chosen position forward and to windward of the mizzen mast and slightly abaft the wheel. He was an old-timer, a Cornishman, who had been sailing these waters for thirty years and was reckoned to know every creek and inlet from Cadiz to Alexandria and to have sailed every strait from Bonifacio to Doro. His experience and knowledge would be invaluable in the shallow coastal waters of Spain.

Near him, by the taffrail, stood McNeil, the first lieutenant, another man well past his prime and the only officer with whom Penhaligon had managed to exchange more than a dozen words. He was a Scot, a dour man but not unkindly, who looked, from his grey hairs and bushy eyebrows, to be all of fifty although ship's records showed him to be five years younger. He had greeted Penhaligon at the entry port with reserve but no obvious resentment that a newcomer, a man young enough to be his son, had been appointed. Penhaligon went forward and stood beside him now.

"We'll be hard put to clear the bay by nightfall at this rate," he observed.

"Aye, but if the breeze holds, sir, it'll likely freshen and we'll have a soldier's wind within the hour."

"I hope so."

McNeil was right. The breeze was strengthening; he could feel the coolness on his cheek and in a moment heard the welcome sound of billowing canvas as topgallants, topsails and courses filled. Looking up, he saw, and was unaccountably moved, by the sight of so many sails straining against the web of ropes, trapped, like errant clouds, against the deep blue of the sky. She was a fine ship.

"Isn't that *Mallorca*, sir, over there to starboard?"

McNeil's question came like a whip of cold spray, reminding him that in his pride he had almost forgotten his old ship.

There on the starboard bow, at no more than three cables' distance, lay the gallant little sloop of war which had been his home, his pride, his means of fulfilment for two long years.

24

She was tiny, almost insignificant seen from the high quarter-deck of the frigate, but no ship of comparable size had achieved more. She still bore the scars of battle. There beneath the chain plates was an area of new timber where the ship-wright had patched her up. Part of the larboard bulwark was also new, and he could see, even at this distance, the plugs and caulked seams which hid further scars. The rigging was new, and a mainsail still had to be bent.

"She's not much to look at," McNeil observed, but, as Penhaligon realised, he meant it kindly.

"No. She's not much to look at."

"I only hope, sir, that *Avenger* achieves as much."

"Thank you, Mr McNeil. That was handsomely said."

As *Avenger* bore down on the sloop of war Penhaligon looked keenly for other work that needed to be done, a hatch coaming smashed by French shot, a backstay broken, a jagged gap in the larboard rail. Much had been done, and he regretted that he would not be able to stop and congratulate Kendall, the first lieutenant, on his work or on his promotion to *Mallorca*'s command. That would not be announced for a few days yet, possibly not until Lord Keith returned, but he was glad that Nelson, whose decision was hardly likely to be questioned, had accepted his recommendation.

"Larboard a little. Meet her. Steady as she goes!" That was Lubbock, who was clearly not concerned about *Mallorca* although at best they would clear by a cable's length.

"What's happening yonder?" McNeil asked, pointing to the sloop of war. "All hands, sir, unless I'm mistaken. Are they afraid we'll ram her?" He turned quickly and called, "Mr Lubbock!"

"Sir?"

"*Mallorca* seems to doubt our intentions. May I suggest another point to larboard?"

"If you say so, sir." The master was offended. Then, to the quartermaster at the wheel, "Larboard a point."

"No reflection on you, Mr Lubbock," Penhaligon called,

"but we're a big ship compared to *Mallorca*. It won't hurt to make them easy."

He wished he had not had to interfere, especially as he guessed that the activity aboard the sloop of war had nothing to do with a possible collision.

As they approached still nearer he saw the watch below come tumbling out, not for any call to braces or to meet some unexpected emergency, but to cram together along the larboard bulwark—like passengers on an Indiaman, he thought —while the officers, all four of them, lined up on the quarterdeck, and the watch on deck had already found positions on the fo'c'sle head or were scrambling up ratlines to the masthead. He could see Buckton, who had saved his life off Cartagena, Illingworth, who had come from the prison hulks off Portsmouth and had been flogged three times within a fortnight before settling down to become a first-class seaman. Pettigrew, the boatswain, was there and fat Lampard, the sail-maker, Judson and O'Malley and Blenkinsop, the cooper. Conscious of a lump in his throat and afraid that someone would sense his emotion, he gripped the taffrail and looked forward, shading his eyes against the sun.

The two ships were close now, less than a cable's length apart. Someone on the quarterdeck, probably Kendall, shouted and waved.

"Good luck, sir." The words came belatedly across the water.

"And to you," shouted Penhaligon, "and thank you."

That raised a cheer, and someone from the maindeck, it sounded like Blenkinsop, bellowed, "Three cheers for Cocky, hip, hip—"

The third cheer was barely audible, so fast was *Avenger* moving, and by the time he turned and had given a final wave *Mallorca* was astern and the crew no more than dots, barely visible against bulwarks and shrouds.

"A happy ship, sir," McNeil commented, coming to stand beside him at the windward rail.

"I like to think so."

The light was fading rapidly now: Ischia, which, only minutes ago, had glowed like a ruby in the setting sun, was no more than a blob on the ever-shortening horizon. Ting-ting, ting-*ting* went the bell, and as a boy came aft to light the binnacle lamp, Carew, Lieutenant Sir Richard Carew, took over the watch.

The wind had strengthened, as McNeil had predicted, as soon as they were clear of the bay, and, coming on the starboard quarter, sent *Avenger* scudding along with bows dipping and bowsprit throwing spray as far as the quarter-deck. It was exhilarating and refreshing but, with darkness falling, hardly safe.

Carew, an elegant young man who, in the few sentences they had exchanged, seemed to have had difficulty in overcoming some secret humour, came aft now and saluted. "Permission to shorten sail, sir?"

"Carry on, Mr Carew. Get the courses in and double-reef the topsails."

"Aye, *aye*, sir!" There was something in his voice or possibly in his bearing that needed watching, although in this half-light it was hard to tell. Watching as he turned to give the orders, Penhaligon thought that unless he was mistaken it would not be long before he and his second lieutenant were crossing swords.

"All hands! All hands to shorten sail!"

Penhaligon waited, quietly at first, comparing the time the watch below took to come on deck with the seconds he had come to expect as normal on *Mallorca*, then with growing impatience as first one, then twos and threes emerged from the fo'c'sle, yawning, scratching heads, some still dressing.

"Mr Lovegrove!" Penhaligon called. "Is that the best you can do?"

"Beg pardon, sir," Lovegrove, the boatswain called up from the gangway. "They're a bit slow, sir, seeing as how they only just came off watch. Then again, sir, it didn't seem urgent."

"Urgent!" Penhaligon felt the rough metal rasping his hands as he gripped the rail. "Every call for hands is urgent: *every* call!" He waited a few seconds to control his anger and then said, forcibly, "I'll speak to you later, Mr Lovegrove. Now get those men aloft!", and, as the boatswain gave his orders, still without any noticeable sense of urgency, "To-morrow we'll practise some sail drill."

Groans and a few muttered curses came from the darkness.

"Silence!" Penhaligon shouted. "Mr Lovegrove, the name of any man who opens his mouth." An unreasonable order, he knew, and impossible to enforce, but it made him feel better. He stood, watching angrily, as dark figures climbed the shrouds.

"Well done, sir," said a voice behind him, and, turning, he saw Carew's grinning face.

"When I want your congratulations, Mr Carew, I'll tell you."

McNeil stood in the dark, a lonely and plainly troubled figure by the after rail. Penhaligon went across to him and said, stiffly, "Mr McNeil, I am going to my cabin. I'd be obliged if you would join me."

"Aye, aye, sir."

He turned, without waiting for the older man, and stumped to the companion. "I'm going below, Mr Carew. Call me if the wind changes."

Once inside the cabin, which in the lamplight looked uncommonly snug and secure, he felt ashamed of his anger. He had come to *Avenger* late, with immediate sailing orders, and had only been aboard an hour or so. It was unfair to judge anyone, least of all the officers, on such short acquaintance.

"Come in!" Bending his head, which he did now automatically, having stunned himself a dozen times on the deck beams of *Mallorca*, he opened the door and welcomed his first lieutenant. "Come, take my chair," and, as McNeil hesitated, "I prefer the cot."

McNeil came in awkwardly, for there was not much room and, even when seated, the captain seemed to take most of it. "One moment," Penhaligon said, and went to the door. "You'll take a glass of wine with me?"

"With pleasure, sir."

"Here, you," he called to the marine sentry. "What's your name?"

"Lapsley, sir."

"All right, Lapsley. Pass word for my steward and tell him I want him in my cabin."

Scarcely had he closed the door than it was opened again by Baghot, who dumped a tray on the table and, without waiting to be ordered, poured two glasses of Marsala. "Here y'are, sir." He thrust one glass at McNeil, another at the captain. "I'll be in the galley, sir, if I'm wanted—only got to shout." He shut the door with a bang, and they heard him exchange some pleasantry with the sentry before shuffling forward.

Penhaligon concentrated on his wine. How could you explain after such a brief acquaintance, especially when the subject of discipline was in the air, that Baghot and he had been together for all of five years, ever since the Irishman had been saved by the persistence of junior lieutenant Penhaligon from the wrath of the formidable Sir John Jervis, "Old Jarvie", and an unjust flogging? How could you point out that while Baghot was rude and to an extent undisciplined, he was also brave and fanatically loyal? Nor could you recount in a few minutes the boarding of *Aristide*, when Baghot, arms red to the elbows, had hacked and thrust his way through a crowd of Frenchmen to stand with feet astride his wounded captain. In the phrase of the time, Baghot was a "character".

"I asked you to see me," he said to McNeil, "because in the unusual circumstances of my joining *Avenger* I missed what any captain needs and normally has a right to expect, a chance to meet officers and crew and to make a thorough inspection of his ship."

McNeil nodded and drank his wine but made no comment.

"So," Penhaligon continued, "I have to rely on you, on your good offices, your honesty, your concern for *Avenger*."

"I hope, sir, that none of those is in question?"

"On the contrary." Penhaligon smiled. "All I am saying is that without your willing help my task will be difficult— not impossible: few things, in my experience, are impossible —but immeasurably more difficult." He leant forward and raised his glass. "That's what I'm asking, Mr McNeil—your help."

McNeil raised his own glass in response. "Which will be gladly given, sir."

"Good!" They drank, and over the rims of their glasses, exchanged appraising glances.

Penhaligon liked what he saw. In the Scotsman's steady gaze he read loyalty, honesty and, what was even more important on a ship of war, courage. "You spoke to me on deck about *Mallorca*," he said. "You observed that she seemed a happy ship."

"That's right, sir."

"Would you care to make the same observation about *Avenger*?"

McNeil hesitated, although apparently not from any reluctance to meet the question, but rather from a desire to find the exact words. "At present, no, sir, although—" He lowered his eyes.

"Although there's no reason why she should not be: is that what you were going to say?"

"Something like that, sir."

"Can you give me a reason?"

"I would rather not, sir."

"I see." Penhaligon said, "Well, I'll be frank with you, Mr McNeil. I have been in the Navy since I was a boy, although I'm sure my service is no more than a fraction of yours, but I have never seen, and I never want to see again, such an exhibition of indiscipline as I witnessed this evening."

"I agree, sir. It was deplorable."

Penhaligon waited, hoping that McNeil would elaborate. "Was this a usual occurrence, would you say, or was it put on for my benefit?"

"Oh, no, sir!" McNeil was shocked. "They have no reason to resent you, sir—quite the contrary."

Again Penhaligon waited and since he suspected that, despite McNeil's reluctance, they were getting near the heart of the matter he remained silent. Above his head the compass told him that they were on a course west-south-west, the steady pitch and roll indicated a fair wind, while the sound of Carew's footsteps above, to and fro, to and fro, as he traversed the quarterdeck was reassuring.

"Would I be right, Mr McNeil," he asked at last, "if I suggested that your reluctance to discuss ship's discipline has something to do with your late captain?"

"I would rather not say, sir."

Penhaligon nodded. "Well, loyalty I can admire."

McNeil remained silent.

"Only look, Mr McNeil: I must know. If I'm to take *Avenger* into action, it is necessary that there should be understanding and confidence between captain and crew and between officers and captain: you must see that."

"Yes, sir."

"Unless I can get to the root of the trouble, whatever it is, your life and mine, the lives of all the crew may be in jeopardy. Whatever went wrong in Chisholm's time, for God's sake let us put it right."

He waited hopefully, but McNeil's eyes were steadfastly on the deck.

"Will it help," Penhaligon said at last, "if I give you my word as an officer and gentleman that no word of any comment you may make will be repeated outside this cabin?"

McNeil raised his eyes. "It will help, sir."

"Good! One more thing: you know, better than I, that

Captain Chisholm is a sick man. He was wounded, badly wounded, at St Vincent; since then, as I understand it, he has contracted what may prove to be a mortal disease." He said, gently, "Captain Chisholm will never command a ship again."

McNeil nodded. "I am sorry, for he was a good officer."

"Was?"

"Before St Vincent, sir. In my opinion, although it's not for me to say, he should never have retained command. He was a good man, none better, but even the best captain is human."

"He received a head wound, I believe?"

"Which changed him, sir. You have never seen a man, a good man, so changed."

"I'm sorry. And this led to indiscipline?"

"He had a morbid fear, sir, of mutiny. The events at Nore and Spithead and aboard *Hermione* preyed on his mind— for no reason, if I may say so, for he had a good crew, and the events of which he heard only came to him second or third hand."

"How did it affect him?"

"Well, sir, in the strangest and most unfortunate way possible. Instead of stricter discipline which, in my view, was unnecessary but would have at least been logical, he decided to placate the men—at all costs."

"Which unsettled them, I imagine?"

"Yes, sir. At first they were just confused. When Lemmon, one of the bo'sun's mates, broke into stores and got drunk on the officers' wine, he was hauled up next morning for punishment, but instead of the flogging which everyone, including Lemmon himself, expected, he was given a mild lecture, and the captain, trying to pass it off as a joke, remarked that it was unfortunate for Lemmon that he had stolen one of the older and more potent wines."

Penhaligon nodded. He had served under easy-going captains before, as well as under martinets, and there was no doubt in his mind that despite the occasional injustice and even cruelty it was the martinet who had the happier ship. "So the crew became restless?"

"Yes, sir."

"What about the officers?"

"Well, sir, that was the difficulty. While Captain Chisholm tried to curry favour with the crew, refusing punishment, allowing them to respond to 'All hands!' in their own good time, he was hard on any officer who tried to impose his own ideas of discipline. Even Lovegrove, the bo'sun, as you saw this evening, became disillusioned until—I've heard it said in the wardroom, although not to me—it was hard to know who was running the ship, captain or crew."

Penhaligon shook his head as he reached across and poured more wine. "There'll be changes from now on, Mr McNeil: I promise you that."

"Yes, sir: I'm glad." He took a sip of wine. "They'll all be glad, sir, crew as well as officers, although some of the crew may resent it at first."

"No doubt. Well, the remedy will be in their own hands." He heard the striking of two bells. *Avenger* was still steady on her course. Above the creak of deck timbers he heard the familiar harp of wind in the rigging.

"You're happy with the crew, I imagine, no trouble-makers?"

McNeil thought for a moment. "Well, sir, there's one. Maybe it's unfair to mention it, since he may turn over a new leaf when he finds the new captain means business. On the other hand—" He stroked his chin. "Maybe you should be warned."

"If you please."

"It's a man called Larsen, sir, a Swede—to be more accurate, Swedish father and Scottish mother."

"That should make him a good seaman."

"So he is, sir, a topman, one of the best."

"But he's a trouble-maker?"

"He's a huge brute of a man, sir; likely you saw him on the starboard watch."

"Tall, bigger than me and twice my weight, with blond hair?"

"That's him, sir. Larsen, the trouble-maker. The men are afraid of him, the midshipmen too, and I'd not swear for some of the officers."

"I'll look out for him."

"He was on *Inflexible*, sir, or so he says, and was one of the crew who fired on *San Fiorenzo*. It's hard to understand why he was not hanged."

Penhaligon leant on his cot with his back against the bulk-head. His eyes were heavy, and the wine, which the British officers had sent up from the royal vineyards in Sicily, was strong. There had been an hour still to dawn when Baghot had wakened him that morning, on another ship, with another command, and the whole day, which included a duel, an interlude for love-making and an interview with the admiral, before him. Tomorrow? He wouldn't think of that yet.

He must have fallen asleep, for later, when he opened his eyes, and, after he had eased the crick in his neck, focused on the compass, he found that McNeil had gone and Baghot, with surprising gentleness for such a bulky man, was undressing him.

"What time is it?"

"Five bells, sir, in the graveyard watch. Wind's moderate, east by nor'-east, sky's clear and Mr McNeil's compliments and he'll call you if there's any change."

"Thank you." He lay there in his shirt, for it was too hot for a blanket, and before Baghot had moved quietly to the door he was asleep.

THREE

THE wind died in the night and when he came on deck, a little after dawn, there was scarcely enough to give steerage way.

It was a fine, clear morning, the sun, mist-covered as it cleared the horizon, gave promise of a scorching day, and the calm, gently undulating sea reminded him of the rise and fall of a woman's breast. He stood for a moment on the main-deck and looked forward where a solitary gull, perhaps injured, perhaps more persistent than its fellows which had long since returned to land, perched on the fo'c'sle head. Four bells were sounding on the quarterdeck.

"Good morning, Mr Hardcastle." As he cleared the companion he touched his hat in response to the fourth lieutenant's salute.

"Good morning, sir."

Penhaligon took up the slate which bore the rough log of their progress through the night. Four knots, four and a half, reducing gradually, as the wind dropped, to three, then two and a half. He held his face to the breeze, or what there was of it, and looked up at the limp canvas. When the next hourly casting was made, and he could see the leadsman now climbing into the chains, the reading would be less than two, the minimum necessary for the helmsman to hold a course. He glanced at the traverse board, which showed the *Avenger* had kept steadily on a bearing west-south-west.

"How's she holding, Mr Rennie?" he asked.

"Hardly at all, sir," the quartermaster replied. "If the wind drops any more we'll be becalmed."

Penhaligon nodded. "Do your best, then. Keep her steady while you can."

He went across to the officer of the watch, young Hardcastle (he was relieved that he had remembered his name), a fresh-faced boy who blushed as the captain spoke to him. "How long have you been commissioned?"

"Two months, sir."

"This is your first ship?"

"Yes, sir. I was guinea-pig aboard *Queen Charlotte.*"

"Under Admiral Lord Keith?"

"Yes, sir."

"Well, you had a good training."

"Yes, sir." The young man looked up at his captain, who towered head and shoulders above him, and, blushing even more, said, "And, sir, if I may be so bold—from what I've heard—I count myself fortunate that I can now serve under you."

Penhaligon looked at him sharply, but there was no hint of insincerity in that ingenuous gaze. "Thank you, Mr Hardcastle. I hope I shan't disappoint you."

He turned to the midshipman of the watch, a dark-haired lad with a lively expression, who was standing by the lee rail, and beckoned him across. "What's your name?"

"Keegan, sir. Please, sir, I'm the signal midshipman."

"Very well, Mr Keegan. I'd be obliged if you'd pass a signal to the bo'sun and tell him I'd like to see him on deck."

"Aye, aye, sir." The boy saluted, ran forward, miraculously avoiding the ringbolts and slides of the quarterdeck carronades, and, after clearing the companion ladder with one leap, disappeared below.

"Tell me, Mr Hardcastle, what would you do in circumstances like these if it came to a bow chase?"

"Sir?"

"We're becalmed, or as nearly so as makes no matter. What would you do if you wanted to close on an enemy?"

The young man looked thoughtful, licked his lips, made

as though to speak, and then hesitated.

"Come, I'm not trying to catch you. Just tell me what you'd do."

"Well, sir. We could wet the sails."

"Good. And suppose that didn't work, suppose there was no wind at all?"

"Then, sir, I'd have the launch and cutter lowered away and start towing." He hesitated a moment and added, "If it was my ship."

"Well done," Penhaligon said. "I'm delighted to find that we think alike."

He had scarcely time to notice the young man's pleasure before Lovegrove, the boatswain, stood before him, saluting. "You wanted me, sir?"

"Yes." Penhaligon pointed to the aft rail where they would be out of earshot of Hardcastle and Keegan and the quartermaster at the wheel.

"Hope you'll forgive my appearance, sir," the boatswain said, "but I was shaving." He looked, and obviously felt, embarrassed with one half of his face smooth, the other black with stubble.

"I understand, although I would have expected you on deck before this. As I read ship's orders you are not required to take a watch?"

"No, sir, except when there's an officer sick or wounded."

"Which is not the case now. We have our full complement."

"Yes, sir."

Penhaligon waited, remembering, and perhaps copying, the way Nelson had attacked with silence when he, Penhaligon, had been called to account for his actions.

"If you please, sir, Captain Chisholm—"

"Mr Lovegrove!" Penhaligon said, forcibly. "Captain Chisholm is no longer in command of this ship. His ways, good or bad, are not necessarily mine. Is that understood?"

"Yes, sir; sorry, sir. I only meant—"

"For instance," Penhaligon interrupted, "why are the watch

37

on deck idle? This deck, and, even worse, the maindeck, are a disgrace. When were they last holystoned?"

"Beg pardon, sir," Lovegrove said, miserably, "two, no three, days ago."

"At what time?"

"Sir?"

"What time of day were they cleaned?"

"The watch after this, sir, when the men had had their breakfast."

Penhaligon nodded and, with hands clasped behind his back, leant forward. "Well, listen to me, Mr Lovegrove, and listen well. In future, quarterdeck and maindeck will be holystoned every day—*every* day: do you understand?"

"Yes, sir."

"And they will be holystoned by the watch of deck, with the help of any defaulters, before four bells in the morning watch. Is that understood?"

"Yes, sir."

Penhaligon said, grimly, "There will be some changes in this ship, Mr Lovegrove; I promise you that. I intend to have discipline, instant discipline, and I intend to have *Avenger* the smartest, aye, and the most successful ship in the Navy. Is that understood?"

"Aye, aye, sir." Poor Lovegrove seemed near to tears.

Then Penhaligon relaxed. He straightened, so that he was no longer bending towards the cowering boatswain, and said, "Very well, Mr Lovegrove, so long as we understand one another."

Unexpectedly, he smiled. "Now I propose to forget everything that has happened since I came aboard and I shall judge you and the crew on what happens from now on. Is that fair?"

Lovegrove swallowed with difficulty and ducked his head. "Yes, sir, thank you, sir—more than fair."

"Then we'll shake hands on it."

That day, the first full day of Penhaligon's command, was

one which no one on *Avenger* would ever forget. After breakfast, with the ship becalmed, everyone was called on deck,
topmen, waisters, gun crews, surgeon's mates, sailmaker's
crew, loblolly boys. At the cry of "All hands! All hands!" the
pipes shrilled, men, urged on by the shouts and rattans of
their petty officers, surged from the fo'c'sle and the main
hatches and formed up facing aft. Penhaligon, by the quarterdeck rail, looked down at more than two hundred faces and
thought with pleasure and a certain amount of relief that his
talk with Lovegrove was already having effect. No one seemed
anxious to fall foul of this fire-eater.

Except one.

"Ship's company assembled, sir."

"Very good, Mr McNeil." He looked down at the crew
and was deciding what line he should take so that no one in
that motley assembly of ex-convicts, vagrants, port lay-abouts
and simple labourers could misunderstand, when he saw a
figure, tall, blond and built like a giant, emerge from the
fo'c'sle.

"Mr McNeil!"

"Sir?"

"You reported company assembled, I believe?"

"Yes, sir."

"Then, may I ask what that seaman is doing forward? He
is, I presume, one of the ship's company?"

"Yes, sir. I beg your pardon, only—"

"Mr Lovegrove!" Penhaligon shouted. "Bring that man
aft."

The boatswain and his mates went forward, uncertainly
it seemed, and approached the latecomer, but their interven-
tion was unnecessary. Ignoring them, the blond giant strode
aft until he reached the waist where the assembled crew, who
only a minute before had seemed crammed to the limit in the
confined area, parted miraculously to give him passage.

The seaman stopped and stood looking up at the captain
with an expression which although not actually insolent was

39

still far from respectful. Penhaligon let him wait a full minute in silence.

Then, "You heard the call for 'All hands!'?"

"No, sir." The man spoke loudly, as though to an audience, and Penhaligon, realising that this was to be a trial of strength, remained calm. "Didn't hear, sir, because I'm a mite deaf." His face was expressionless, but Penhaligon did not miss the nudges and half-smiles among the crew.

"Nor did you hear the whistles?"

"No, sir."

Penhaligon controlled himself with difficulty, knowing that if he indulged in any show of temper now he would have lost. He also sensed the clash between main and quarterdecks, no doubt fostered by this man, the crew wanting their comrade to maintain his defiance, the officers willing the captain to be firm.

"Where were you five minutes ago?"

"In the fo'c'sle."

Penhaligon gave him a few seconds' grace, then shouted, "Sir! You call me 'sir'."

He was glad to note that this sudden thrust had taken the seaman by surprise, for he looked markedly less confident. "In the fo'c'sle, *sir*."

"Then you saw the rest of the crew coming aloft."

"No, sir. I was asleep, or, at least, resting—having done the morning watch."

"I see." The big man was uneasy now, Penhaligon was glad to note. His eyes as he looked up to the quarterdeck and into the sun were uncertain. "You are a topman, I believe?"

"Yes, sir."

"So your berth will be by the companion."

There was a long silence before the man answered. "Yes, sir."

"And you are telling me that you neither saw nor heard the rest of the crew running out of the fo'c'sle, pushing, talk-

ing, stepping over you and even on you, I shouldn't wonder?
Is that what you are saying?"

The topman remained silent, and Penhaligon knew that
he had won. "Very well," he said. "Fall in," and then,
"Master-at-arms, take that man's name. We'll see what a
spell at the gratings will do for his hearing."

He waited for the ranks to open and enclose the now
discomfited Larsen—for this, undoubtedly, was McNeil's
trouble-maker—before he addressed the crew.

"I am your new captain," he said. "Penhaligon is my name,
and since we are going to be together for some time it's only
right that you should know my intentions."

He paused and was glad to see that he had their attention :
two hundred faces were turned towards him.

"In my old ship, which was smaller than this, although
whether you're in a tiny brig of war or a first-rate ship of
the line, the same principles apply, I insisted on efficiency.
In insisted on my ship being as smart and well run and as
efficient as any ship in the Navy—and a good deal more
efficient, I would say, than any Frog or Spaniard.

"Efficiency comes from hard work and discipline—aye, and
pride. You men have got to be *proud* of *Avenger*, you've got
to believe that there's not a better or a more dangerous fighting ship in these waters, and, by God, when you believe that
we'll prove it."

As he spoke, although he was taking in the whole scene,
the foremast and jib boom almost stationary against the
horizon, the seagull which, like an omen, good or bad, refused
to desert them, he was conscious of their reactions and he felt
a thrill as he saw their eyes brighten and even heard a
subdued cheer.

"We'll have a lot of fighting to do, lads, in the next few
months, and I'm looking to you to prove what we all know,
that one English Jack is worth six or seven Frogs or—what?—
a dozen Spaniards?"

"Two dozen, sir," someone called, and raised a cheer.

"They may have bigger ships than *Avenger*, but that don't matter; we can sail faster and manoeuvre more quickly, so we'll have them like a terrier at a bull's tail. We'll take prizes, for in these waters there are still fat merchantmen about. I'm promising nothing, but there's no reason, if you play your part, why we shouldn't all be rich, and when the war is over you will go home with enough money to buy a farm or a shop or an inn or whatever your fancy pleases, and, looking back, I'll wager you will thank God that we were efficient."

They cheered now without restraint, for even the suggestion that this war could ever end and that at some time in the not impossible future Napoleon would be defeated was a hope they had scarcely dared cherish. Home, even a tumbledown cottage or a slum in Whitechapel, was a nostalgic dream.

Penhaligon nodded and smiled. "Good! Now, as you can see, lads, we are becalmed. No Frogs today or prizes, so we are going to take a look at this efficiency: sail drill this morning and gun drill after dinner—since there's no wind to kill, it won't hurt to loose off a few rounds.

"You'll sweat today, I promise you, and there'll be some, perhaps most of you before the day's out, who will be wishing me dead. But remember that this is the first time I'll be seeing you, and I must know what you can do. Make it your best, lads, and tomorrow, if we get a wind, we'll go after the Frogs."

He turned to the sound of their cheers and nodded to McNeil, who was looking at him with open admiration. "Carry on, Mr McNeil. I suggest we have tops'ls and yards struck, all top hamper down and stowed away."

"Aye, aye, sir."

The only slight irritation to mar his pleasure was the look on the face of his second lieutenant. It was there for a moment, as their eyes met, and as quickly vanished, but he knew that whatever McNeil or any other officer might think, and despite the new-found enthusiasm of the crew, Lieutenant Sir Richard Carew had no illusions—he recognised Cocky

The English Captain

Penhaligon for what he was, a glib, self-assured young man blessed with physique, courage and abundant energy and, what was even more useful, a persuasive charm which he could turn on and off at will. Popular with women and, by all accounts, a more than satisfactory lover, he was also, by Carew's standards, a bit of a cad.

43

FOUR

"SAIL HO! Sail on the starboard bow!"

The cry from the maintop, coming after three days of calm seas and empty horizons, was like a message of hope. The watch on deck, a loblolly boy with bucket resting on the lee bulwark, the sailmaker threading needle with twine, paused in their labours and looked out over the measureless blue of sea and sky as though by some miracle what was barely visible through a telescope from a position seventy feet above their heads might also be seen from deck with the naked eye.

On the quarterdeck, Carew, the officer of the watch, looked upwards, shielding his eyes against the sun, and shouted, "Maintop there! What do you see?"

"A ship, sir, close-hauled, looks like a merchantman."

"Very well." Carew turned to the midshipman of the watch. "Tell the captain."

In fact it was not necessary. As Penhaligon came on deck he was met and all but knocked from his feet by the flying body of Midshipman Keegan vaulting down the companion. "Beg pardon, sir." The boy, who in his anxiety to miss the captain had tried, unsuccessfully, to alter course in mid-flight, picked himself up and saluted. "Very sorry, sir. Didn't see you. Hope you're not hurt."

"You didn't hurt me, boy. What about yourself?"

"No damage, sir, and, if you please, sir, maintop reports sail on the starboard bow."

On the quarterdeck, Carew touched his hat and offered his telescope to the captain. "Nothing yet, sir, but with this wind on the quarter it shouldn't be long."

44

Penhaligon nodded and, after several sweeps of the glass, saw what appeared to be a smudge on the horizon. He looked up and shouted, "Maintop! How is she making?"

"She's wearing ship, sir—must have seen us."

"What do you make of her?"

"Please, sir, she's hull down, but I see her mastheads. She's square-rigged, sir—looks like a brig."

Penhaligon looked at Carew. "Set all sail, if you please. We'll take a look."

"All hands! All hands to make sail! All hands!" As the pipes shrilled, the watch below came pouring out to join their comrades on deck in racing up the ratlines, out by the futtock shrouds, and, with only the meagre support of footropes, along the swaying yards where royals were loosened and studding sails set. *Avenger*, responding, dipped her bows to the waves and then threw up her bowsprit, sending a flurry of spray aft, while the symmetrical pyramids of canvas, straining against sheets and tacks, arched against the sky.

"What do you think, sir?" Carew asked. "Is she a Frog?"

"It's possible. We are still only a short haul from Sardinia. On the other hand, she could be Algerine. We're no great distance from Barbary."

Carew smiled—without sympathy, it seemed to Penhaligon—and observed, "A ticklish problem, sir, if she's flying the flag of Islam. It wouldn't do to offend our allies."

He was right. The Barbary Coast, from Cyrenaica to Oran, was ruled by minor potentates, all warlike and not far removed from pirates, who, owing nominal allegiance to the Sultan of Turkey, were Britain's allies. The advantage was all one-sided. While a British ship dared not attack the flag of Islam, the Algerines plundered any European vessel that caught their eye, provided the odds were right, and were known to hold hundreds of unfortunate Christians in slavery.

The distance between the two vessels was closing fast. She was hull up now, even from the maindeck, and through his glass Penhaligon could see the square sails, still set on a

45

diverging tack, although this signified nothing since, unless she turned and ran before the wind, she had no chance of escaping.

"What do you make of her, sir?" Carew asked.

"She's a merchantman, all right: European built."

"So she could be a Frog?"

"It's possible. We'll soon know."

With the wind on the quarter, *Avenger* raced onwards. By the weather rail Penhaligon watched the jib boom rising and falling against the horizon as, with a crash of waves and a cascade of foam, she plunged her bows into the sea and, with scarcely a roll, came up with masts a-tilt, throwing water over the fo'c'sle head and into the scuppers. Down–up, down–up. Forward on the maindeck, the watch, ready at braces, steadied themselves against stays and stanchions and, with spray in their eyes, watched the chase.

Feet astride, bending his knees to the sway, Carew was looking through the glass. "Unless I'm mistaken—yes—I thought so." With a smug expression he handed the telescope to the captain. "Hard luck, sir! They're Islamic colours. Shall I call off the chase?"

Penhaligon did not reply. Through the glass he could see the brig quite clearly now, the crates on the maindeck and the two officers on the poop wearing Arab burnous and caftans. The helmsman and the two seamen forward wore what seemed to be European clothes, but this probably meant that they were slaves or captives from some merchantman.

"Get the stuns'ls in," Penhaligon ordered, "and lay a course alongside."

"Aye, aye, sir." Carew sounded disappointed. "Hands to braces! Hands to shorten sail! Larboard a point, Mr Rennie."

Coming from windward, *Avenger* was closing fast: through the telescope Penhaligon could see no untoward activity aboard the brig, no sign of panic. It was not until *Avenger* turned into the wind that he was able to read the name abaft the beakhead: *Lyon*.

He passed the glass to Carew. "That's an odd name for an Algerine."

"A captured ship, sir, one they took from the French."

"Perhaps."

"Make the private signal, if you please." It was not likely that a ship of such a doubtful ally would have been given the code, but it was possible.

Keegan, at the halliards with the sail-locker open, was already passing flags to the signal rating. In a moment—too quickly by far, Penhaligon thought—the brig ran up a reply.

"Correct, sir, by the new code," Keegan shouted.

Carew shut his glass and slipped it into his pocket. "Looks as though our chase was for nothing, sir."

Penhaligon continued to stare at the heavily laden brig. He wasn't satisfied. Despite the Islamic flag and the Arabs on the quarterdeck, despite the deck cargo and the coded reply, there was something wrong. She lay low in the water, he noticed, and even on the larboard tack the sea was only a few feet below the tumblehome.

"Signal her to heave-to."

"Sir?" Carew stared at him in amazement. "Do you think we are justified?"

"Do as I say."

He could understand Carew's doubts, in fact he shared them himself. The Dey of Algiers was not likely to be pleased if one of his merchantmen was intercepted, and all kinds of complications could follow, diplomatic protests, even more depredations by his lateen-sailed gallivats, at worst, severance of the so-called alliance. Although the Turks and Algerines were no practical use in England's struggle against France and Spain, it was comforting to know that they were not on the other side.

"Signal acknowledged, sir," Keegan shouted.

Penhaligon waited. The more he saw, the more suspicious he became, although he would have been hard put to explain his unease. More crew had come aloft now, he saw, and were heaving at topsail braces: they all wore European clothing.

"Heave-to, Mr Carew, if you please. Lay her alongside."

With topsails backed, the two ships drifted together until they were no more than a long stone's throw apart. The brig had reduced the hands on deck again to two: for some reason the Algerines were unduly shy.

Penhaligon took up the speaking trumpet and shouted: "Where are you bound?"

The Arabs on the quarterdeck exchanged glances and shrugged.

"They don't understand, sir."

He tried again, in French: "*Où allez-vous?*"

Again there were shrugs of incomprehension.

"Mr McNeil," Penhaligon said to the first lieutenant, who had just come on deck. "Is there anyone aboard who speaks their lingo?"

"No, sir. I'm afraid not. There's only Larsen, who speaks Swedish."

"That's not much help."

He stood, gripping the taffrail, while he pondered his lonely problem. If he boarded her and was proved wrong he could expect a court martial and, at best, a reprimand. On the other hand, England was at war: he had a duty. Then, as he stood, a prey to uncertainty and conscious always of the officers behind him—McNeil, who would back him, he thought, right or wrong, and Carew, who clearly thought he was mad—he remembered something Nelson had said to him in that big, ornate room in the Capodimonte Palace. "Always go at 'em," the little admiral had said, which, as Penhaligon interpreted, meant, "When in doubt, attack."

"Mr Carew," he said, "give the order to lower away the cutter and have a boarding party stand by. I'm going aboard."

"Aye, aye, sir." If Carew thought his captain was crazy or at best ill-advised, he was too well trained in naval discipline to show it. "Mr Lovegrove," he called. "Lower away the

cutter. Pass word to Mr Dexter that we'll want half a dozen
of his marines."

Penhaligon took up the speaking trumpet again and
shouted : *"Arrêtez-vous là ou je vais vous envoyer au fond!"*
He comforted himself with the thought that if they really were
Algerines and could not understand French they would be
unaware that he had threatened to sink them.

"I'm going across, Mr McNeil," he said. "If I'm not back
in half an hour you'll know what to do."

"Aye, aye, sir." The first lieutenant accompanied him to
the companion and, apparently at a loss for words, merely
nodded and said, "Good luck, sir."

At the entry port a section of marines led by a heavily
moustachioed sergeant stood to attention, muskets by sides,
while below, a dozen seamen, each armed with cutlass and
dagger, sat by their oars. Glancing downwards, for despite all
his efforts he still could not remember names of more than
half the ship's company, he recognised Simmons, the coxswain,
at the tiller, Baghot, who would not willingly forgo even the
half-chance of a fight, Ellery and Lamont and, to his great
surprise, Larsen. He wondered how the Swede had come to
be chosen, for although he was clearly the man to have in
a fight, his shoulders, if not his dignity, must still be smarting
from the twelve strokes he had received only yesterday.

Following the marines, he went down the ladder, waited for
the boat to steady and then, with one foot on the gunwale,
stepped into the stern-sheets. He nodded to the coxswain.
"Give way!"

Pulled by twelve stalwart oarsmen, of whom Larsen, showing no obvious discomfort, was one, the cutter moved smoothly
across the water. The sun was hot, he could feel it scorching
his back, and the bare arms and faces of the oarsmen, already
nut brown, were running with sweat.

Soon the brig was towering above them, and as they came
under the stern he saw the name more clearly: *Lyon.* He
saw, too, that masts, rigging, bulwarks and well-pitched hull

were all in good shape. If this ship had been seized from the French, it had been taken without a fight.

"Easy!"

As the coxswain fastened to the main chains Penhaligon, closely followed by the marine sergeant, leapt on to the ladder and climbed to the entry port.

The maindeck, so far as he could see, was deserted. The crates, stacked higher than the bulwark and occupying most of the maindeck from fo'c'sle to waist, were, on closer inspection, packed with arms. Some, marked *Danger!*, appeared to hold powder, while others, sixty, seventy, possibly a hundred crates on the starboard side alone, of which one, near the entry port, was open, contained muskets. Further aft, in the well of the maindeck, were artillery field pieces, carriages, trunnions, barrels, all neatly laid and ready for asssembly at some foreign port. The two Arabs were still on the poop.

Drawing his sword, Penhaligon walked towards them.

He suspected a trap. Whether they were Arabs or Frenchmen, he could think of no reason why the crew should hide below. If they were Frenchmen held by a handful of Algerines they would surely have uttered some cries for help as they crouched in the darkness below hatches. But there was silence. The men he had seen at the braces were European; of that he was sure. The answer lay on the poop deck.

As he climbed the companion with sword drawn and the marine sergeant at his shoulder, he saw the two officers slip off their burnous and reveal themselves as Europeans.

The taller man, apparently the captain, bowed and said in good English, "Welcome aboard, captain. It seems that our little comedy is over."

"I'm afraid so. My name is Penhaligon of His Majesty's frigate *Avenger*. May I trouble you for your sword."

"The English Captain!" The Frenchman looked at him with new interest as he unbuckled his sword. "It is an honour, captain, to be taken by such a worthy foe."

"Your name, sir?"

"What? Oh, I beg your pardon. My name is Lacoste, Captain Lacoste, and may I present my second in command, Lieutenant Auber?"

Penhaligon bent his head to acknowledge the lieutenant's bow. "And the crew?"

"Are Frenchmen to a man, sir, as you see."

The Frenchman smiled as he said this and waved towards the larboard bulwark where, miraculously, a number of crates had opened to reveal a score of seamen with muskets covering the poop.

"As you will see," Lacoste said, raising his voice so that the Englishmen, who were confined to the narrow space between pyramids of crates on the starboard side, could hear, "if anyone should be so foolish as to attack, the first one to be shot will be the captain." As he said this he re-buckled his sword.

"May I also point out," he said, "that the crates beside you contain powder. One shot from my men and you will be blown sky high."

"Together with you and your ship," Penhaligon replied, just as loudly. He looked down at the marines who, in their scarlet jackets, were crammed together with a number of field pieces into the well of the maindeck, and at the seamen—he noticed Larsen standing head and shoulders above the rest—to starboard. "Don't be afraid, lads," he shouted. "If they shoot, they'll blow themselves up as well as you."

With a cry, the Englishmen surged forward, led by a red-faced and highly incensed Baghot. There was a skirmish in the waist in which the marines with bayonets fixed fought the French, who, now that their bluff was called, had to use their muskets as clubs.

"Get 'em, lads!" Penhaligon called, seeing no point in adding to the confusion on the maindeck. From his position at the rail he had a grandstand view.

At first the Frenchmen, joined by more of their comrades from below, held their own, but, faced by the sweating, swearing marines and the yelling seamen, among whom

Larsen was always prominent, they retreated. Forward to the main hatch they went, fighting desperately over crates and coils of rope and stacked canvas; then to the fo'c'sle. At last, apart from a wounded Frenchman moaning quietly to himself in the scuppers and another, lying across a crate, who appeared to be dead, the maindeck was empty.

Penhaligon turned with a sigh of satisfaction and found himself looking into the barrel of a pistol.

"Don't count your chickens, captain," Lacoste said. "Isn't that the saying? You may think you have won, but I still hold a trump while I have you."

"Don't be a fool, Lacoste," Penhaligon said, as he pushed the pistol aside and walked to the taffrail. "Admit defeat and come aboard as my prisoner. If you harm me now, you'll hang." He looked over the side, thinking that if necessary he would have to take an unwanted swim. It was a long drop to the water below.

"I won't have to harm you, captain, if you do as I say," Lacoste replied. "Get your men off my ship and let us proceed. I give you my word as an officer and a gentleman that you will be released on parole when we reach Alexandria."

"So that's where you are going. Succour for the lost army! Is Boney still dreaming of India?"

He spoke tauntingly, hoping to make the Frenchman angry, and as he saw the tell-tale flush on his cheek he leant back against the rail and suddenly kicked with all his force towards the crotch.

Lacoste dropped his pistol and doubled up, his face twisted with pain. Hobbling with knees together and feet apart, he moved round awkwardly, like a clockwork doll, uttering anguished cries. Lieutenant Auber, who clearly had no taste for a fight, kept himself to himself by the forward rail.

It was several minutes before Lacoste could bear to pull himself upright, and by that time the victorious British were coming aft along the maindeck. "Sir!" Lacoste said, his face still twisted with pain. "You are no gentleman."

Penhaligon shrugged. "I'm afraid you are right, sir, but see what advantages it gives me."

He went to the companion and looked down at the boarding party. Most were breathing hard and smiling broadly, although one or two were nursing wounds. Larsen, whose shirt had been ripped off, had a knife wound across his chest to offset the less honourable scars on his back. As he met Penhaligon's eyes he was smiling.

"Well done, lads," Penhaligon cried. "There'll be prize money in this for all of you." He looked, and it was only then that he realised that someone was missing. "Where's Baghot?"

"Coming, sir!"

After five years, nothing Baghot did could surprise him—or so he thought.

"Found this in the cockpit, sir," his steward said, pushing into the crowd of marines and seamen. "Thought you'd be interested."

"This" was a pretty young girl of sixteen or seventeen with red lips and smiling eyes who looked up at the quarterdeck, clasped her hands together, and cried, "Cocky! Cocky Penhaligon!"

FIVE

SHE had a pert face of the kind the French called *gamine*, with pointed chin, a ready smile and eyes that were both alert and mischievous. When she saw that he had failed to recognise her, she ran up the companion and, to the delight of the watching crew, leapt—for her head barely reached his shoulder—and, clasping arms round his neck, gave him a resounding kiss.

"Ma'am." It was not often that he was put out of countenance by a woman, but he was conscious not only of the crew, but of the two French officers at his back. Even worse, he could not, try as he would, remember her.

"Ma'am, I am sorry. You have the advantage of me."

She smiled even more broadly. "Shame on you, then, for Baghot remembered. Greystone Park, your last leave in England—remember?"

At once pictures formed; *Prince George*, home from the West Indies, Penhaligon, the third lieutenant, with no home, no relations apart from a crusty old uncle in Cornwall, invited by the second lieutenant to share his leave. Greystone Park, a fine old house set in acres of parkland : he remembered the deer and the sheep and the Highland cattle, he remembered his host, Rear-Admiral Sir Hubert Campden, and his son, Penhaligon's shipmate, Jamie. And—everything was coming back to him now—there had been a sister, a saucy chit of a girl, who put sand in his porridge, holly in his bed and, at the ball given in their honour, pinned a card to his back so that he went down to meet the assembled guests with a notice proclaiming : "The worst dancer on the floor."

"Clarissa!" he cried. "Good God! Clarissa Campden!"

"And you'd forgotten!"

"But that was three, nearly four years ago." He put his hands on her shoulders to look at her. "You've grown."

She laughed. "Well, now that I've found you again, I shall continue to torment you. For you'll take me on your ship?"

"Of course." He found it hard to marshal his thoughts. "But how on earth—? No, never mind: time for questions later. You are, I take it, a prisoner?"

"A very troublesome prisoner, I'm afraid."

"You have been well treated?"

"Oh, yes." She looked demurely at the French officers, who were standing rather self-consciously apart, by the binnacle. "Captain Lacoste is a gentleman."

"So I understand!" Penhaligon turned and said, "Captain, I must ask you and Lieutenant Auber to accompany me to *Avenger*. I need hardly say that you will be treated, as prisoners of war, with every respect."

The Frenchmen bowed, Lacoste with some difficulty, and proceeded to the entry port.

"Sergeant!" Penhaligon called. "I'm leaving you and your marines in charge. I'll have you relieved shortly."

He took Clarissa's hand—she really was a pretty girl—and said, "Come! I'll show you my ship."

She sat beside him in the stern-sheets, her eyes lively and enquiring, missing nothing, the French officers in the thwarts, the four crewmen who had been wounded making light of their disabilities, although one was clearly in some pain, and the remaining oarsmen pulling steadily, so that in no time at all the cutter was alongside *Avenger* and the coxswain was tying up at the entry port.

"We'll need her again directly, Mr Simmons," Penhaligon said. "See that these wounded men are given a hand. Those that want to can see the surgeon." He knew, without being reminded by their expressions, that no wounded man who could stand on his own two feet would willingly put himself at the mercy of the saw-bones. A few days on light duty, wounds bathed in seawater and, within a week, they would be well.

"Come!" He held out his hand and assisted her to the ladder, which she ascended like a tomboy, with a flurry of skirt and petticoats and no apparent thought for the appreciative eyes of the seamen below. On deck she stood for a moment, looking around, and then, before Penhaligon could join her, rushed forward, past the startled McNeil, and threw her arms round Carew.

"Richard! Of all the luck!" She repeated the kiss she had earlier bestowed on Penhaligon.

"Clarissa! I can't believe it!"

"No need for introductions," Penhaligon observed, sourly. "You two obviously know each other." If he felt a trifle put out, he told himself that it was only because of his vague uneasiness with Carew. "Clarissa, may I introduce my first officer, Lieutenant Andrew McNeil."

"Mr McNeil!" She bobbed a curtsy, and for a moment, as she lowered her gaze, Penhaligon found it hard to remember that she was not the demure miss she seemed.

But there were other things to consider and a number of decisions to make. The two Frenchmen were waiting.

"Mr Simmons!" he called. "I'll trouble you to escort Captain Lacoste and Lieutenant Auber to the cockpit. They are to be made as comfortable as possible and to be treated with respect at all times."

"Aye, aye, sir."

"And, captain," Penhaligon said. "It would give me pleasure if you would join me for dinner."

Lacoste bowed stiffly and said, "Thank you, captain, but with your permission Lieutenant Auber and I would prefer to dine alone."

"As you wish."

He watched them go below, Lacoste still limping, and said,

"Well now, the first thing is to complete our intelligence. Clarissa, we must rely on you."

"I'll do my best."

"Good." He thought for a moment. "Mr McNeil, I'd like you to be present; you, too, Mr Carew."

"Aye, aye, sir." McNeil asked, "Where shall we gather, sir? May I suggest the wardroom?"

"Thank you, Mr McNeil. That would be excellent."

Clarissa, as the only woman aboard and a remarkably pretty one at that, was sure of their attention, but, so charmingly did she talk, sitting facing them across the wardroom table, that even McNeil, who as a middle-aged Scotsman and a sailor, had no great opinion of women, was enchanted.

"First," she said, "since I doubt that you know, Daddy has been appointed Flag Officer Commanding Minorca."

"Splendid!" Penhaligon remembered him well and hoped that the admiral, who had seemingly had no great opinion of him as a third lieutenant, would have mellowed. "And Jamie?"

"Is there, too. In a few days, if we avoid any more adventures, you will see him."

"I shall look forward to it. What rank does he hold now? I assume he's on your father's staff?"

She hesitated. "Well, no, although—well, you'll see. In fact, Jamie has left the Navy."

"Left the Navy!" Penhaligon beat his hand on the table. "I don't believe it."

"Well, it's true. I'm sure Jamie will explain."

Penhaligon nodded. There was something strange here, something he didn't understand. The Campdens had been sailors for generations.

"So, tell us what happened," he asked. "How, in heaven's name, did you come to be a prisoner of the French?"

She smiled and shook her head. "You'd never believe. Minorca was tiresome. I don't know whether you have put in there since we captured it, but there's nothing to do, no

57

social life, no young people, so—" She gestured with her hands. "I asked Daddy if he would send me to Naples."

"Why Naples?"

She looked at him from under her lashes and said, "Do I have to have a reason? Because you were there, perhaps—and Richard."

"All right." Penhaligon grinned. "That's as good a reason as any."

"Well, there was a sloop of war *Diogenes* leaving almost at once. She was carrying mail and supplies, and even without favourable winds Daddy expected her to make a fast passage."

"What happened?"

"The second day out of Minorca we ran into a storm. We shipped a good deal of water—I tell you, it was quite frightening—and the mainsail was ripped to shreds. While the crew were bending another sail, masthead reported two ships on the horizon."

"*Lyon?*"

"And her escort, a French ship of the line."

"*Gironde?*" Penhaligon gave it as a statement rather than a question, so sure was he that the fortunes of *Avenger* and the French ship were interlinked.

She looked at him in surprise. "You knew?"

"Our mission," McNeil explained, "is to seek out and destroy *Gironde*. We assumed she must be in these waters."

"But she's a ship of the line, while you—" She hesitated.

"Are a 32-gun frigate," Carew said, with feeling. "I hope you'll explain that to your father."

"I hope you won't," Penhaligon said, sharply. "We can and will sink *Gironde*."

She looked at him and grinned mischievously. "What a fire-eater!"

"Beg pardon, sir," Baghot said, knocking and entering without bothering to wait for permission. "Two Frogs are in the cockpit, sir. Made 'em as comfortable as I can. Now, sir, I was wondering about the young lady. Can I get her some refreshment?" He shuffled self-consciously and blushed as Clarissa smiled at him.

"That's very kind of you, Baghot. I would like some wine."

"Madeira, Miss, or claret, or perhaps you'd prefer a glass of Marsala? Then there's some ham and pease pudding, and—"

"Baghot!" Penhaligon interrupted. "We are very busy. I am anxious to get *Avenger* under way. Now just bring us a bottle of Marsala and some glasses and leave us alone. I am hoping that Miss Campden will do me the honour of dining with me."

"Aye, aye, sir," Baghot replied, quite unabashed. "As long as you'd not forgot."

Penhaligon turned to Clarissa again, although not without catching the glances that passed between McNeil and Carew. "What happened next?"

"Well, it was inevitable, I suppose. *Gironde* left the ship she was escorting and engaged us. There was no fight: *Diogenes* was in no position to defend herself. *Gironde* sent aboard a prize crew. I, as the only female aboard, was transferred to *Lyon.*"

"Why *Lyon*? Why not *Gironde*?"

"There was no room, or so I was told. In the four days from Barcelona, *Gironde* had taken three British ships, including a brig of war."

"That would be *Persephone*," Penhaligon said. He drummed his fingers on the table. "And she did all this while she was supposed to be escorting *Lyon*?"

"Yes."

"So she was off on another chase when we arrived?"

"I suppose so. It was my good fortune."

"And she'll return as soon as the chase is over."

"Yes, do you think—?" Suddenly Clarissa was serious, realising perhaps that she might have been too sanguine in thinking that her troubles were over.

"Baghot!" Penhaligon yelled, with such force that they

59

were all startled, and as the door opened, "Belay whatever you're doing and take a message to the quarterdeck. Tell Mr Hardcastle, with my compliments, that I want double look-outs posted at masthead. Tell him to ask the bo'sun for the best men he's got."

"Aye, aye, sir."

"And, Baghot!"

"Sir?"

"At the double."

He leant forward in his chair with his arms on the table and for a moment forgot Clarissa and McNeil and the hand-some Carew, forgot the heaving deck and the protesting timbers as *Avenger* rolled. Soon, much sooner than he had dared hope, the battle would be joined. Morale was high, he had felt that on his daily inspection forward and at divisions, and would be higher still after the capture of *Lyon*. He had a good crew, and *Avenger* was faster and more manoeuvrable than any ship of the line. All he wanted was a chance.

"What?" He realised that McNeil was talking.

"I was asking about your plans, sir."

"I'll tell you. You, Mr Carew, will take a prize crew aboard *Lyon*. You will set course for Minorca and, as quickly as possible, get under way. If this wind holds, you can be there in two days, three at the most. Get Lubbock to give you your position."

Carew watched him in silence for a moment, with the hint of a sardonic smile. "You want *me* to go, sir?"

"Yes." Penhaligon stirred uneasily. He disliked having to explain his decisions, but in this case, with the aristocratic young lieutenant's eyes upon him, he felt he should. "I'm sending you rather than Hardcastle because I think it needs an officer with experience. The cargo of *Lyon* is important, to us as well as the French: they aren't going to let it go without a struggle."

"A charming prospect!" Carew commented. "Sailing a strange ship, full of powder and with a skeleton crew, while the enemy ship of the line uses us as target practice."

"It won't be like that. Use your head, man! Why should they send a shipload of guns and ammunition to the bottom when Napoleon's army in Egypt is desperate?"

"True," McNeil said. "That's a point."

"So you think they'll let us sail into Mahon without a fight, sir?" Carew asked.

"On the contrary. They'll attack you, try to capture you —but that's what we want."

"What *you* want," Carew muttered.

"What we should all want," Penhaligon insisted, "since it will give *Avenger* the chance to engage *Gironde*—which, if I may remind you, was the reason we were sent to these waters."

Carew stood up. "Very well, sir. If those are your orders. And since I can leave Miss Campden, whose family if I may remind you, sir, are old friends, in your capable hands I shall go with a clear conscience."

Penhaligon glared at him but made no reply. Perhaps it was true, as Carew obviously thought, that one reason why he had chosen the second lieutenant rather than the most junior officer was jealousy. Carew's acquaintance with Clarissa had been longer and perhaps more intimate than his own: and she *was* a pretty girl.

But what Carew, or Clarissa herself for that matter, would never understand was that seamanship and the ship he commanded came before everything. The Duchess of Potenza, Emma Hamilton and a score of other beautiful women were important to him at the time: he made love easily and was faithful after his fashion: but no woman had, or ever would, come before his ship.

SIX

Wɪᴛʜ a fair wind and all sails set, *Lyon* headed towards Minorca. From *Avenger*'s quarterdeck Penhaligon watched as she pitched and rolled through moderate seas, with masts swaying and the great spread of canvas, from flying jib to driver, straining to push the heavily laden ship through the water. She was not built for speed, even under favourable conditions, and with foredeck awash to every pitch, and the bulwarks, on the roll, scarcely clear of water, Carew would be lucky if he managed three knots.

"She's making heavy weather, sir," McNeil said, as he stood with the captain on the quarterdeck.

"Yes." Penhaligon felt a growing frustration, since with a wind that would push *Avenger* to seven, or even eight, knots he was forced to reduce canvas to topsails and double-reefed courses so that they would not surge ahead of their ponderous charge. "I said two, possibly three, days to Mahon. It's more likely to be four."

"At least, sir, there's no sign of *Gironde*."

Penhaligon nodded. With *Lyon* in their hands and shadows lengthening, there was much to be thankful for. On the other hand, he could not believe that the French would give up their valuable cargo lightly. Things were going badly for Napoleon, despite land victories over the Austrians and Russians. The army stranded by Nelson's victory at the Nile could not be abandoned.

"The young lady seems to have settled down, sir," McNeil said. "Let's hope for her sake *Gironde* doesn't find us."

His remark, which was kindly meant, irritated Penhaligon.

He had almost forgotten Clarissa, although from his position by the weather rail he could see her head and shoulders as she read, or pretended to read, a book under the canopy Baghot had fixed for her on the maindeck. Whether the book —it was a manual of seamanship—was not to her liking or whether she was unable to think seriously of anything for long, it seemed whenever he glanced in her direction that she was more interested in the activity on deck, the sailmaker with his canvas, the gun crews at drill and the watch manning sheets and braces, than in her reading. Her pert, lively face and her obvious interest were much to the liking of the crew who frequently—much too frequently, Penhaligon thought— glanced in her direction and performed their duties with a swagger which he found most irritating. Women and ships did not go together: he had always felt that. Separately he loved them both, but the worst hell he could imagine was to be captain of a female-infested Indiaman.

"Sail ho! Sail on the starboard quarter!"

The cry from masthead brought him sharply from his ill-temper.

"Masthead! What do you make of her?"

"Can't tell properly, sir. She's big, hull down. I can just see topgallants and royals."

"I'll take a look." Even more irritated by the thought that Clarissa was watching, he climbed the mizzen shrouds, through the lubber's hole, ignoring, because of her, the more spectacular route by the futtock shrouds, until he reached the mizzen topgallant masthead.

"She's coming up now, sir," said Larsen, who was sitting astride the topgallant yard. "I can see her tops'ls. Looks like she's seen us."

Penhaligon swept his glass across the horizon. There she was, a big ship, for in this light, the brightness before dusk, she must be all of twenty miles away. Royals, topgallants and topsails were square on, and he could just see the curve of her staysails. *Gironde* without a doubt, and under full canvas.

"Is she a Frog, sir? Is she coming after us?"

"Let's hope so." Penhaligon smiled, for after the salutary lesson of the flogging Larsen seemed a new man. He had fought well on *Lyon* and seemed to bear no ill-will. "Let me know what she does and give me a call when she's hull up."

"Aye, aye, sir."

Penhaligon looked down at the drop of more than a hundred feet to the deck. On the quarterdeck the foreshortened figures of McNeil and the helmsman and the midshipman of the watch looked slightly absurd, like gnomes in a cabbage patch: only Clarissa, with her dress spreading across the deck, looked graceful.

Penhaligon shook his head: it was always harder to climb down than up. He said to Larsen, who was still seated nonchalantly on the yard, "You've a better head for this than I have."

It was another hour and the sun was already touching the horizon before *Gironde* became hull up. Although the light was good, she was still not visible from deck without a glass, and Penhaligon knew that she would be all of fifteen miles away when darkness fell. He considered altering course with the thought of losing her in the night, but even if this were possible, and he doubted whether *Gironde*'s captain would fall for that old trick, he deemed it wiser to press on with all speed, realising that for the moment his duty was to get *Lyon* and her valuable cargo to safety. Also he would not have the French think that he was running away.

"Ting-ting, ting-*ting*." Time for the watch to change. Meldrum, the third lieutenant, touched his hat to the quarterdeck. *Lyon* was still ploughing along half a mile to starboard.

McNeil cleared his throat. "Would you like me to stay on deck, sir, at least until dark?"

"No, thank you, Mr McNeil. I'll be here for a while yet. You go below and get some rest. It's likely to be a long day tomorrow."

He settled down at the starboard rail and watched the brig

still making heavy weather, although Carew, quite rightly, in view of approaching darkness, had shortened canvas. Without taking his arms from the rail he saw Meldrum, who seemed a sound if unspectacular officer, studying the slate and traverse board. Forward, on the maindeck, Baghot was offering Clarissa a mug of his unspeakable coffee. Astern, long since lost to sight but still, he knew, pursuing, was *Gironde*. He smiled with anticipation. Tomorrow would certainly be a long and, he hoped, a rewarding day.

"Beg pardon, sir."

He turned from his thoughts to Baghot, who was now only visible as a shape in the darkness, so quickly had night descended. "What is it?"

"The young lady, sir, asks if she can see you."

"Up here?" He shook his head. "No, I told her I couldn't have her on the quarterdeck."

"Not here, sir, in the cabin."

"What? Oh, very well." Clarissa had been installed in his cabin, while he had taken Carew's quarters. "Do you know what she wants?"

"To say good night, sir; at least that's what she said."

His scowl was lost on Baghot, who stood aside, whistling softly through his teeth, as the captain went below.

The lantern was already alight outside his cabin, but the sentry, who normally stood there, was missing.

"Sentry!" he called, angrily, and then almost collided with him as he turned a corner of the passage.

"Beg pardon, sir, I'm here—just doing my rounds."

"Very well." He felt, and probably looked, foolish. According to ship's orders, the sentries should patrol the passages to starboard and larboard as far forward as the main hatch, although in fact more often than not they spent most of the time leaning against the bulkhead by the captain's cabin. "Carry on."

He knocked at the door, which was opened, almost at once, by Clarissa.

"Come in!"

"No. I can't stay. I just came to see if you were all right."

"Oh, come in!" Before he could protest further she had grabbed his arm and dragged him with such force that he cracked his forehead on the lintel.

"Steady!"

"Oh!" She put her hands to her mouth and watched him with concern, although he saw, to his annoyance, that her lips were struggling against a smile. "I'm so sorry."

"Are you?" He said, still rubbing his forehead, "You haven't changed much, have you? I remember you as a skinny, particularly obnoxious little girl in long frilly drawers. Now that you've grown up you've stopped being skinny, but you're just as determined to torment me."

"You're wrong," she protested, "quite wrong. I don't want to torment you, Cocky—that's the last thing I want to do." She put on her mischievous smile. "And I don't wear long frilly drawers."

"So I see." He sat on his cot and looked at her with an expression of resignation. Nobody could stay angry with her for long. Because she had had to leave *Diogenes* with nothing more than the clothes she was wearing, she had attired herself for the night in one of his shirts. The sleeves she had rolled to the elbows, but the rest was so big that the tails hung below her knees, and the neck, which she had not troubled to button, kept slipping from her shoulders. She looked, in the dim light of the cabin, entrancing.

"You look like an urchin," he said. "If only your father could see you now."

"Heaven forbid!" she said, and came to sit beside him.

He heard the bell by the binnacle struck twice and Meldrum give some order to the helmsman. Under reefed topsails *Avenger* moved steadily through the night.

He stood up. "I must go."

"Oh!" She reached up and took his arm. "Not yet. Stay for a while." He shook his head. "Half an hour?"

"No."

"Fifteen minutes?"

"No."

"Five?"

With a sigh that was more an admission of defeat than a sign of frustration, he sat down again. "Very well: five minutes."

She grinned with pleasure and rested her head against his arm. "Oh, Cocky, I do love you."

"Clarissa!" He was surprised more than shocked. In society, in Clarissa's society, young ladies did not talk so frankly, although, as he put an arm round her shoulders, he had to admit that Clarissa was different. "You shouldn't say such things, although don't think that I'm taken in. I know this is one of your tricks."

"No, Cocky—honestly! I mean it. I've always loved you, from the very first day when I saw you coming up the drive with Jamie."

"As I remember, you had a strange way of showing it."

She laughed and snuggled even more closely into his arms. "That was just my teasing, because you wouldn't look at me."

"I was probably shy."

"No. You were right. I was an obnoxious child."

He looked down at her and stroked the hair from her face. "I could hardly have known then, could I, that you would grow into such a beautiful young lady?"

"Oh, Cocky!" Her voice was small. "Do you mean it?"

"No, I'm only teasing." His shirt had slipped from her shoulder completely, and he rested his hand on her breast. It was soft and warm, and beneath it he could feel her heart beating. "I mean it," he said, and kissed her on the lips.

"Cocky, darling!" As she fell backwards on the cot the shirt slipped to her waist, and she made no attempt to cover herself as she reached out her arms.

Later, as they lay side by side, watching the swinging shadows and the compass point hovering around nor'-nor'-

west, she said, "What I said this afternoon was true, Cocky—
about my reason for going to Naples."

"To see Richard Carew, that's what you said."

"I was teasing: you know I was teasing. I don't even like
Richard, and I love you."

"How did you know I was in Naples?"

"I hear lots of things I shouldn't now that Daddy is flag
officer commanding."

"I suppose so."

"Some things I heard made me even more determined to
see you."

"About *Mallorca*? Yes, well, we had our successes. She
was a good ship."

"Not about *Mallorca*."

"What, then?"

She turned her head and moved slightly away from him.
"About other women, two in particular."

"Emma? Emma Hamilton?"

"She was one."

"And Maddalena?"

"I don't know." She was more upset than he had thought.
"The Duchess of something or other."

"Duchess of Potenza, that's right." He raised himself on
to one elbow and looked down into her hurt, elfin face. "They
are friends, Maddalena and Emma—just friends."

"That's not what I heard."

"Well, you know all about gossip. Out here, especially in
Naples, there's nothing else to do."

"Cocky." She put her hands on his shoulders. "Look at
me. Swear that neither Emma nor this Maddalena was ever
your lover."

The words, the usual glib assurances, formed on his lips,
but seeing the tears in her eyes and the downward tilt of her
lips, he found to his astonishment that he could not bring
himself to say them. He shook his head. "I can't."

"You see!" Her face puckered up and she was really crying.

"Clarissa!" He knelt over her and tried to make her look at him. "Don't cry. Clarissa, there's no need. Please don't cry."

But she couldn't stop. She turned her head on the pillow, and lay still, but not resisting, as he made love.

It was not long, though, before she responded, and her tears had stopped as, at last, she came to the orgasm. Clasping her arms around him, she cried out and then pressed her lips to his.

In a minute he drew away and, with an unaccustomed tenderness, stroked her face. "Whatever I have done in the past, Clarissa, you must forget. None of it means anything to me now—I swear it. There's only one person I love, Clarissa: I love you."

As he felt her arms around him and the softness of her body, he remembered how many times he had been through this scene before, using the same words, or others like them, making the same appropriate gestures and responses. "But this time," he thought, in astonishment, "is different. I *mean* it."

SEVEN

HE WAS on deck an hour before dawn, although with a heavy sea running and the wind almost gale force on the larboard quarter he did not think that *Gironde* would have closed on them during the night. None but a reckless captain would keep a big two-decker under more than minimum canvas during the hours of darkness, and although he knew that Lamartin, the captain of *Gironde*, was resourceful, he did not think that he was reckless. Visual contact had been maintained with *Lyon* all night, and it was reassuring to see her red larboard light flickering like a glow-worm in the dark. The heavy pitch as *Avenger* plunged into the waves cut a line of creaming foam to meet and join the combers which ran alongside, and the whole of the quarterdeck was repeatedly drenched by spray.

Balancing himself against the rise and fall of the deck, feeling the sting of cold seawater, and hearing the wind howling in the rigging, Penhaligon felt exhilarated. Today, unless he was mistaken, they would engage *Gironde*.

"It will soon be dawn, sir." Hardcastle was clearly relieved that in these conditions and with a French ship of the line somewhere in the offing the captain had come to share his responsibility.

"What time is dawn?"

"Five twenty-one, sir."

Forty minutes, although in these conditions visibility would probably be limited for an hour or so.

"Who's aloft?"

"Craxton, sir, one of the topmen, and Mr Lacey."

"Good!" It was just as well to have two look-outs, and the eyes of a keen young midshipman were likely to be sharp. He was intensely anxious to know what dawn would bring.

In fact, it was something of an anticlimax. As the dawn sky astern became tinged with grey, visibility extended to the maindeck, where, despite the drenching spray and the water running through the scuppers, the watch were on hands and knees with holystones, then to the gangway and the fo'c'sle and the aggressively pitching jib boom; then, as the grey merged with gold, to the angry, white-capped sea. *Lyon* was visible now, still under topsails and topgallants, and from the amount of water breaking over her bows Penhaligon guessed that Carew would soon have to reduce canvas still further.

"Masthead!" he shouted. "What do you see?" His cry was swallowed up by the wind, and he had to repeat it through the speaking trumpet.

The replies by the midshipman at the mizzen masthead and Craxton on the maintop were equally lost, but he saw from their gestures that there was nothing.

"Good morning, sir." McNeil, who was probably as anxious as he was to see the dawn, although for a different reason, had come on deck more than two hours before he was due to take over the watch.

"A time for patience," Penhaligon observed. "It will be an hour yet before we can see more than a couple of miles."

"Probably more, sir, if I may suggest. At least we can still hope that *Gironde* is not on our tail."

In fact they were both wrong. McNeil had scarcely gone below to take an early breakfast before the low cloud dispersed, and, as the horizon retreated, Midshipman Lacey, at mizzen masthead, cried, "Sail ho! Sail on the starboard quarter!"

Penhaligon took his glass and trained it on the horizon, and almost at once picked up a blob, which appeared, on focusing, to be a ship, hull up, carrying all top canvas and main course.

"I think it's *Gironde*, sir."

So, the chase was on. Quarry and hunter had scarcely changed positions in the darkness.

"Can you see her, sir?" McNeil was thrusting an arm into his jacket as he climbed the companion.

Penhaligon passed him his glass. "There, hull up. She must be twelve or thirteen miles away."

"How long before she catches us?"

Penhaligon turned the figures over in his mind. Assuming *Gironde* had an advantage of four knots, she would be within range in three hours; if the advantage was only three knots they would have another hour: it depended on how much canvas *Gironde*'s captain was prepared to risk.

"Send the men to breakfast, Mr Hardcastle, if you please. Mr Keegan, signal *Lyon* 'Enemy on starboard quarter'." It was unlikely that Carew would have missed sighting their pursuer, although with a strange ship and a skeleton crew he would have plenty to occupy his mind.

"Coffee, sir." Baghot held out the steaming mug as though bestowing a gift, and stayed to see that the captain took at least a sip. "Young lady sends her compliments, sir, and if you're not actually engaged in fighting the enemy would you join her for breakfast?"

Clarissa! Even in the exhilaration of impending battle he could still feel an extra thrill as he thought of her. 'If you're not actually engaged in fighting the enemy'! He grinned and handed the mug back to his steward. Why not?

His day cabin, which was even smaller than the confined area where they had made love last evening, contained a table, half covered with maps, ship's orders and sextant, and a couple of chairs. It was, as Clarissa observed, cosy. While Baghot served them with wine—Penhaligon refused to insult Clarissa with coffee—biscuits, butter and ham, they kissed and held hands and made love with their eyes until the sounding of eight bells, the change of watch, brought Penhaligon back to duty.

"I must go."

"Of course." She held his hand as he rose, not to detain but rather to maintain physical contact until the last possible moment. "Is there anything I can do?"

"Just keep yourself safe, that's all I ask. I'm afraid that when we clear for action I shall have to ask you to go to the cable tier. Baghot will look after you." He kissed her hand. "It won't be comfortable, but at least you should be safe."

"Don't worry, darling. I've experienced worse. On *Diogenes* they put me in the orlop."

On deck, even before he climbed the companion, he saw that *Gironde* was clearly visible. The wind had abated a little, although the sea was still flecked with white-caps, and *Lyon*, which was still carrying the same canvas, plunged fussily along.

"*Gironde* is coming up fast, sir," McNeil said, as Penhaligon joined him on the quarterdeck. "She's now carrying all her courses."

"Yes, another hour, possibly less, and we'll go to meet her."

It was an exercise in trigonometry, the kind he had worked out time and time again in the seclusion of his cabin. Force and direction of the wind, the amount of canvas carried and from this the relative speeds, the distance between the two ships: these were the variables, and one could only make a provisional plan based on the factors at the moment and the probable change of variables. Ideally, *Avenger* would engage *Gironde* a mile or so astern of *Lyon*; she would attack from windward, preferably out of the sun, and from such an angle that the French ship would be denied in that first encounter, while gun crews were fresh and barrels cold, the possibility of a telling broadside. It was a time for cool heads.

In fact, another hour passed before Penhaligon thought it necessary to alter course. There was no point in having the crew ready too soon, for there could be no one aboard who was not aware that before the day was out *Gironde* and *Avenger* would be engaged in a death struggle.

"Hands to wear ship!"

From the speed with which hands ran to braces and the smooth, almost copybook turn before the wind, Penhaligon knew that, despite earlier misgivings, the crew were efficient. He looked across at *Lyon*, which was already pulling away, and called to the signal midshipman, "Mr Keegan! Send a message to *Lyon*: 'Good luck!' "

Gironde was coming directly at them now on an opposite course and at a distance of perhaps two miles. With all sail set, including stunsails, she was a magnificent sight, and, so parallel were their courses, the three masts, with their spread of canvas, appeared as one. There was still a heavy sea running, and the bow wave was clearly visible every time she dipped her bows.

"Clear for action, Mr McNeil, if you please."

"All hands! Clear for action! All hands!"

The shouted order and the drum roll were merely signals to set the well-rehearsed drill in motion. The crew came pouring out, marines, gun crews, topmen, waisters; decks were doused with water and sanded; water buckets were placed by guns and at the mainmast. At each hatch a marine sentry stood with fixed bayonet to deny passage below, while in the captain's cabin and the wardroom bulkheads were being knocked down to accommodate gun crews. Down in the cockpit, from which the unfortunate French officers had been escorted, the surgeon's mates were moving the sea chests of junior officers to form improvised beds. The gunner and his mates, wearing slippers to avoid the possibility of sparks, were on their way to the magazine from which in a few minutes the powder boys would come running with their charges. At the guns, breechings were cast off and the crew were ready at tackles for the order to load and run out. The gunner, who mistrusted the new-fangled flintlock mechanism, had already given orders for slow-burning matches to be lit so that, if his worst fears were realised, gun captains would be able to light their linstocks.

"Ship ready and cleared for action, sir."

"Very good, Mr McNeil. Up ports and run out guns."

The two ships were coming together quickly now. *Gironde* would also be cleared for action, only she had seventy-four guns to oppose thirty-two, and she had the weather gage.

"Wear ship!"

There was clearly no chance of gaining the weather gage, and he could only consider the possibility of manoeuvring so that, when the ships met, *Gironde* would be denied the full advantage of her station. With thirty-two pounders on her gun deck and twenty-four pounders on the main, not to mention the sixty-eight pound carronades on her quarterdeck and the long-tom in her bows, she had enough metal to cripple *Avenger* with one broadside, and, with the wind on her quarter, Lamartin would be anticipating two or even three broadsides before the advantage was lost.

As *Avenger* came round into the wind, close-hauled on the starboard tack, he saw that *Gironde*, following, had come helm a-weather so that the two ships were on converging courses. Lamartin, no doubt, intended that they should remain so, for as soon as *Avenger* was within range his gunners would have time to lay accurately, fire, swab out and reload, and still have time for at least one more broadside. He wondered how accurate were her gunners.

"Guns loaded and run out, sir."

He turned from his deliberations to Meldrum, the gunnery officer, who was standing before him, grim faced and sweating a little, no doubt from the effort of visiting and inspecting the flintlocks, lanyards, tackles, quoins and breechings of thirty-two guns.

"Very well, Mr Meldrum. Await my order to fire."

"Aye, aye, sir."

"And, Mr Meldrum, have the carronades loaded with canister. Tell the carronade captains to fire as they bear."

Meldrum hesitated for a moment, but made no comment. "Aye, aye, sir."

Penhaligon clasped his hands behind him, aware that he had surprised Meldrum, and probably McNeil, who was standing only a yard or so away. Canister was a horrible weapon, throwing a hail of musket balls into a relatively confined area and causing, if the carronade was accurately laid, multiple wounds and disfigurement. It was, of course, one of the accepted horrors of warfare, but in England's long struggle against Napoleon, British and French officers had generally engaged one another with gallantry, and there was a kind of gentleman's agreement that neither side should depart, unless it was considered absolutely necessary, from the rules of civilised conduct.

Well, thought Penhaligon, we are fighting against the odds and we are fighting to win.

"Mr Dexter! Pass the word for Mr Dexter!"

The captain of marines came aft at the double. In his scarlet tunic with gleaming buttons, white breeches and shako he looked absurdly out of place on a ship of war, but he was, according to McNeil, a bonny fighter. "Two marksmen, Mr Dexter, the best you've got—up in the main shrouds. Tell 'em to look out for *Gironde*'s captain."

"Aye, aye, sir."

There was no point in half-measures. If, by chance, the two ships came close enough for carronades to be fired with any degree of accuracy, and this meant something less than a hundred yards, it was possible that by killing some officers or, even better, the helmsman, *Gironde* could be put at a disadvantage. The two marines in the shrouds were no more than a gamble, for, from the insubstantial foothold of the ratline, even at a hundred yards it would need more than a measure of good luck to score a hit.

"The wind's abating, sir," McNeil observed.

"So it is, by God!" Only minutes ago, it seemed, he had been buffeted by sudden gusts as it shrieked through the rigging and along the decks. Now, although still strong, it was steady and possibly diminishing.

He knew then what he would do.

"Mr McNeil, unless the wind strengthens again, I propose at the appropriate time to give the order to go about."

He saw, and indeed had expected, McNeil's look of consternation, for it meant that even before the battle was joined he was proposing to put *Avenger* at risk.

To change tack in anything but a calm sea it was customary to wear ship, a long and cumbersome procedure, which involved turning before the wind, squaring off the yards and bracing sharply on the other tack. While *Avenger* was doing this her guns would be virtually useless and she would be a sitting target.

The other, quicker, way, which Penhaligon proposed, involved considerable risks.

"Full and by!"

"Full and by, sir." The quartermaster had her as close to the wind as he dared.

"*Gironde*'s opened fire, sir!" Poor Hardcastle, who had probably never been in close action before, had difficulty in controlling his voice.

"Much good it will do her," Penhaligon replied, as a shot splashed into the sea a cable's length ahead.

He wondered what Lamartin was thinking. A long shot by one of the twelve-pounders in *Gironde*'s bows was probably no more than a boost for morale, for the chance of hitting a narrow, ever-moving target was small. It would be different when *Avenger* showed her beam. Was he congratulating himself on his good fortune in having the much larger ship and the weather gage? If so, a surprise move might take him unawares.

"She'll be opening up in earnest soon," McNeil observed. The distance between the ships was still considerable, perhaps half a mile, but on their converging courses it was rapidly narrowing. Soon *Avenger* would be presenting a more acceptable target.

"For what we are about to receive!" Penhaligon heard

77

someone—one of the midshipmen?—utter the time-honoured blasphemy.

The first broadside fell short by half a cable's length at least and brought a nervous reaction from *Avenger*'s crew. Boos and shouts of derision greeted the line of splashes to starboard and were still sounding as *Gironde*'s gun deck was again wreathed in smoke. This time the aim was better. The line of splashes, forming almost simultaneously to prove that there was discipline among *Gironde*'s gunners, straddled the sea beside the starboard bow and clipped, with a single shot, the hull above the cutwater. Penhaligon clasped hands tightly behind his back and watched the rapidly narrowing distance.

The temptation to fire was almost irresistible. In a moment, he knew, he would have to give the order, if only to relieve tension on deck, but he knew the importance of that first broadside, laid with care and controlled by the master gunner. It was essential to get the maximum effect.

"*Gironde*'s opened up again," Hardcastle shouted.

It was noticeable that the time between sighting the puffs of smoke and the arrival of shot was shortening. There was scarcely two cables' length between the ships now.

Three hundred pounds of metal screamed overhead, tearing holes in the main course and the mizzen topsail and severing one side of the foremast weather shrouds. Only one shot, more effective although clearly less well laid than the rest, tore through the bulwark and scored a smouldering trail across the deck.

"Fire buckets forward! Look lively there! Fire buckets!"

Under the anxious eye of the boatswain, waisters were already throwing water on the deck.

Penhaligon nodded with satisfaction. So *Gironde*'s crew were capable of error, even at this early stage. Someone, the master gunner or, more likely, the gunnery officer, had given the order too late, on the upward roll.

"Mr Meldrum!" he shouted. "Fire as you bear."

There was a noticeable stir among the crew on deck, a

ripple of anticipation, which manifested itself in bright, expectant faces and keen glances towards *Gironde*.

"Fire!"

The starboard guns roared out as one and, in a matter of seconds, so close were the ships, the crew shouted in triumph as holes appeared in *Gironde*'s hull and in her canvas, and she seemed to pause momentarily, like a runner thrown from his stride.

"Swab out! Reload!" Sixteen gun crews were pushing wet swabs down the barrels before ramming in fresh charges and shot. Despite the pall of smoke, which got into lungs and eyes, they strained on the tackles to heave the guns forward where the captain with handspikes under the carriages found their directions and, with adjustments to the quoins, their elevation.

"Cock your locks! Take aim! Fire!"

The two broadsides must have been fired simultaneously, for the deadly hail which tore through *Avenger*'s hull and across the deck, where two seamen were killed, made everyone forget what might have happened on *Gironde*.

"Prepare to go about!"

As he gave the order Penhaligon knew that he had left it as late as possible—too late if *Gironde*'s crew had time to reload and fire another broadside. The two ships were barely a cable's length apart.

"Hands to braces!"

Now was the testing time. If the yards were not turned at exactly the right moment, if she failed to come up into the wind, she would be left wallowing, possibly drifting stern first, until she could gather fresh steerage way. During this time she would be helpless before *Gironde*'s pounding. He refused to think of the even worse damage which could result from a broken stay.

"Larboard your helm!"

He watched anxiously, scarcely conscious of *Gironde*, which, apparently caught by surprise, heeled over and went rushing past in a flurry of foam and with larboard guns pointing skywards.

"Steady!"

With his eyes on the slowly swinging bows he waited tensely, and then, when they came within two points of the wind, raised his hand. At the urgent command from the boatswain, seamen hauled on the forward braces, the yards turned and, to Penhaligon's intense relief, the forecourse filled. The bows were still swinging. He waited until he felt the wind on his left cheek and raised his hand again. Crew at main and mizzen braces now took up the strain, the yards were hauled round, and, having traversed approximately thirteen points of the compass, *Avenger* lay on the new tack and with the weather gage.

Penhaligon looked at McNeil and smiled with relief.

"Magnificent, sir, if I may say so," McNeil said, and meant it.

But the battle had scarcely begun. Now that *Avenger* had the weather station, it was necessary to strike home the advantage.

"Prepare to alter course!"

As *Avenger* swung before the wind, Penhaligon, and indeed the whole crew, noted with pleasure that *Gironde*, having lost the gage, was having to wear to meet the challenge. For a time at least the advantage lay with *Avenger*.

"Steady as she goes!"

The two ships were approaching on collision course, and while *Gironde* clearly wanted to claw her way to windward, *Avenger* wanted to maintain her advantage as long as possible.

"Take in the headsails!"

Bearing down, with the wind on her quarter, *Avenger* had a free choice of manoeuvre. If, as Penhaligon suspected, Lamartin was aiming to accept *Avenger*'s broadside as the price for regaining the windward station, Penhaligon was determined to thwart him. Having taken one risk and won, he was quite prepared to take another.

"Mr Meldrum, have the larboard guns ready. Fire as she turns."

"Beg pardon, sir," the quartermaster called, "but it's going to be a turble close thing."

"So much the better, Mr Rennie. Let's see what these Frogs are made of."

Even from the quarterdeck he could see the bows of *Gironde* bearing down, the high bowsprit and jib boom, the creaming bow wave, and, above, the slanting tiers of canvas. Within minutes the ships, if they maintained their present courses, would meet head-on.

"Helm a-lee!"

He could imagine the consternation on *Gironde*'s quarterdeck. Instead of a close manoeuvre in which the ships would pass on opposite courses, *Avenger*, with the advantage of the wind, was swinging to starboard, which meant that unless Lamartin was prepared to risk a damaging collision he must turn *Gironde* before the wind and expose not only her beam but her vulnerable stern. And *Avenger* would still have the weather station.

"Fire!"

As the two ships came together the broadsides roared out simultaneously, and for a time, on both decks, there was almost total confusion. Almost but not quite : in the swirling, acrid smoke of the guns and with the screams of dead and dying men in his ears, Penhaligon stood calmly watching *Gironde*'s hull moving alongside, at no more than a stone's throw distance, and the near-panic of the French crew as they struggled to douse fires and reload guns and drag their wounded to the hatches. For a time the two quarterdecks were parallel, and he saw Lamartin watching closely, trying to guess, perhaps, what he would do next. At that moment *Avenger*'s quarterdeck carronades opened fire.

He had no time to see what devastation they caused, for there were problems enough on *Avenger*. Two of the larboard guns were out of action, one shot had demolished most of the forward rail, and there was damage to the mizzen stays.

He could only guess what was happening below, and he found himself thinking, amid all the smoke and confusion, of Clarissa waiting, alone and frightened, in the cable tier.

"Mr Lambert's compliments, sir, and there's four shot holes, one below the water line. He's doing his best, sir, to plug them, and he says there's no cause for alarm." The boy who had brought the carpenter's message was breathless, either from fright or from the exertion of running or, perhaps, from finding himself face to face with the captain.

"My compliments to Mr Lambert and tell him I'm sure he will do his best."

Gironde was having to wear : it was the only course left, and as *Avenger* turned in pursuit the high stern was exposed.

"Fire !"

Meldrum's gunners were excelling themselves. Several holes appeared near the water line, and the stern walk, unseated from its stanchions, hung like a broken limb into the sea.

"Well done !" Penhaligon shouted, although with the smell of victory in the air the gunners needed no encouragement.

"Sir !" Something, a desperate note of urgency in McNeil's voice, made him turn. "The mizzen stays, sir. We're near to being dismasted."

He looked up. One or more shots, probably in that last exchange, had severed two of the stays, and the mizzen, already overstrained by his unorthodox manoeuvre of tacking, was listing sternwards.

"You're right, by God ! Get the canvas off her. Mr Lacey, pass the word for the sailmaker."

It was infuriating. Unless the remaining stays could take the strain until the yards were lowered, the mizzen would collapse, and from previous actions he knew that in the welter of spars and ropes and canvas it would be impossible to maintain the action. Even as he looked, *Gironde* was turning across the wind.

"Quickly, for God's sake !"

He muttered the imprecation to himself, well aware that the boatswain and crew were working desperately to save the position.

"Look, sir!" It was Hardcastle pointing forward and calling with a shrill note of relief, "*Gironde*'s pulling away."

It was true. Having made the turn, *Gironde* was changing course again and, with the wind now on her quarter, was breaking off the engagement.

"Damn and blast her! What's she up to?"

"Her main yard has gone, sir," McNeil said, "and unless I'm mistaken she's listing."

"Yes, sir, she is," Hardcastle shouted. "We must have holed her below the waterline."

With a feeling of utter frustration, Penhaligon could only watch her pull away. He saw the mass of wreckage on her deck where yard and rigging and maincourse had fallen. Like *Avenger*, the French ship had suffered a disabling blow.

But he was too near victory to give up.

"Hurry up with that canvas!" he shouted.

"Doing our best, sir," Lovegrove called, his voice taut with anxiety. Royal and topgallant and topsail yards had been lowered; they were just tackling the mizzen peak.

" 'Ware below! She's going!"

He stood quite still, ignoring the danger of falling yards and canvas, as the mizzen mast, unable to stand the strain any longer, broke from its seating and fell in a graceful arc astern, across the taffrail and the nettings, into the sea.

EIGHT

REAR-ADMIRAL SIR HUBERT CAMPDEN, BART, Flag Officer
Commanding Minorca, nicknamed "Cammy" by the King
and "Old Gouty" by friends and subordinates, was a gentleman of the old school. Penhaligon, who had met him only
once, during his stay at Greystone Park four years earlier,
knew that the admiral didn't like him, but hoped that in view
of his friendship with Jamie and the something more than
friendship with Clarissa the old boy would accept him. There
was also the question of *Lyon*.

She had arrived in port that morning, escorted by *Avenger*,
and from the window of the house on Gallows Hill he could
see her now, guarded by a contingent of the Thirty-ninth
Foot, her decks still stacked with crates of arms and ammunition which a civilian assessor, one of Sir Hubert's men, was
examining, and hull and rigging still bearing signs of the
recent skirmish.

"Penhaligon!" Sir Hubert came hobbling in, leaning on his
daughter's arm, and his face and hostile eyes belying the sub-
stance of his greeting. "Glad to see you—my congratulations."

"Thank you, sir." Penhaligon bowed and, despite Clarissa's
mischievous grin, managed to keep a straight face.

"Splendid capture, *Lyon*—valuable cargo—splendid."

"More valuable than the cargo, sir, was the captive we
found aboard."

"Ah, yes—Clarissa." Supporting himself against the table,
he dragged himself to the high-backed chair and, once settled,
glared at his daughter's rescuer. "Grateful to ye, although it

was no more than she deserved—still, I'm glad you got her back."

"Perhaps it will be a lesson to her," Penhaligon suggested, piously. "Perhaps she will accept the wiser counsel of her elders in future."

"What? Oh, quite so." Sir Hubert hurrumphed and shifted in his chair, while Clarissa gave Penhaligon a 'Just you wait!' look.

"I'm very grateful to Captain Penhaligon, too, Daddy," she said, sweetly, "especially as he clearly found me something of an encumbrance."

"What?" Sir Hubert glared at them both from under bushy eyebrows, but it seemed to Penhaligon that he had too much experience of his daughter's teasing to be taken in. "Dare say you were, if it comes to that. Ship of war's no place for a woman."

"Once he shut me in the cable tier."

"During action, sir," Penhaligon explained, hastily, "while we were engaging *Gironde*."

"Quite right, too. Where else did ye expect him to put you —on the quarterdeck?"

"I don't know, Daddy, but if I had been there perhaps we shouldn't have lost the mizzen."

At that Sir Hubert lay back and roared with laughter, although it was clear, from his careful movements and the quick return to gravity, that he was in some pain. It was also clear that he had a deep love for his daughter. "She's got you there, Penhaligon. Trust a woman to have the last word. You did lose your mizzen."

"Not exactly, sir. We recovered it from the sea."

"And lost *Gironde*." He shook his head, but still good-humouredly, "At least ye did better than others that have tackled her, including, I may say, certain ships of the line."

"It was unfortunate, sir," Penhaligon said, "but we'll get her yet. This was just the first round."

"Good, although I hope you know what you've taken on.

Gironde's a powerful ship and Lamartin is a good commander. Nelson clearly thought you could do it, otherwise he wouldn't have sent ye, but the odds are long."

"Lord Nelson was right," Clarissa said, and took Penhaligon's arm. "He knows that Jethro is too good for any Frenchman."

She remained holding his arm, her face flushed, and her eyes fearlessly meeting her father's. For a moment Penhaligon thought that the admiral would erupt, but, instead, after a sharp look at Clarissa and an even sharper look at her lover, he said, "Well, Penhaligon, it seems you have made a conquest."

"If I have, sir, it is one I would place above all others."

Sir Hubert continued to look at them, apparently still not sure of the attitude he should take, but then, with a kindly smile, he nodded to Clarissa and said, "Run along now, child. Penhaligon and I have business to discuss."

"All right, Daddy." She went round the table and kissed him and, as she ran across the room, blew a kiss to Penhaligon. The door closed.

It was a glorious day, Penhaligon decided, the sun was shining, the hill beyond the red-roofed cottages was bright with flowers, and the sea, from the harbour to the distant horizon, was blue.

"Come, let's look at this ship you've captured," Sir Hubert said. "On the way we can talk."

They travelled in an open carriage, Sir Hubert, red of face, wincing every time the wheels ran over stones or pot-holes, and in only a few minutes drew up on the quay. A scarlet-coated sentry jumped to attention and presented arms, and in a few minutes his sergeant came hurrying forward. "Good morning, sir. Cargo's being checked. Mr Murdo's there now, sir, and—"

"Very good, sergeant. Ask Mr Murdo to see me."

The man who now came down the gangway and crossed the quay to Sir Hubert's carriage was a typical civilian assessor, mean, suspicious, narrow-minded. Penhaligon, like other captains before him, sometimes wondered how they were selected. Perhaps, although it seemed unlikely, they were, or had been, ordinary men, with ordinary Christian virtues of tolerance, kind-heartedness, even generosity, and it was the job, the assessment of prize ships and cargoes, that debased them. Directly responsible to the port admiral—in this case, Sir Hubert—they gained, as did the port admiral, from low assessments, which limited the prize monies distributed to officers and crew, and from pocketing the difference between assessment and true value. It was an open scandal which festered in the minds of most captains.

"What's your opinion, Murdo?"

The assessor looked doubtful, guessing that Penhaligon was the captain who had taken *Lyon*. "Well, sir, the ship's not bad, although there's worm in the hull. Masts and rigging are so-so. It depends, sir, whether their Lordships at the Admiralty want her."

"You have your doubts?"

"Yes, sir. You see, sir, she's a brig, old-fashioned—not much scope for ships like her in the Navy."

Sir Hubert nodded and glanced at Penhaligon, whose face was expressionless. "I see. Well, it don't look as though we'll have much of a sale there."

"No, sir. Then there's the powder, sir—poor-quality stuff and not to be relied on. Shouldn't think the Navy would use it."

"And what else?"

"Guns, sir—muskets, although being French and not like the English, I can't see that we could sell them."

"And the field pieces?" Penhaligon asked, in a tight voice. "Weren't there some field pieces?"

"Aye, sir, there were, but then again—"

"They're of French design and you can't sell them," Penhaligon completed. He was furious and he had a feeling that Sir Hubert not only knew it but was secretly rejoicing.

Was this his way of getting his own back on the man who had dared to fall in love with his daughter? Or was he, reflecting his daughter, simply teasing.

Penhaligon leant forward and thrust his face at the assessor who was standing directly beside him. "Mr Murdo," he said, "if that's your name, you may be a good assessor, although I'd need proof of that, but you are certainly a Job's comforter. While you have been sitting in port, in a nice comfortable billet, my men have been out in all weathers, on call night and day with seldom a proper night's sleep; they've been cold and, more often than not, wet through; they've sweated and worked to defend men like you, and with no more reward than food you'd not see fit to give to your dog; they've fought —aye, they've fought well, and many have died." He thrust his face even further forward so that the startled assessor took a quick step backwards. "And if you think I am going to let a fat, mealy-mouthed, hypocritical old skinflint like you cheat them out of their earnings, then you are gravely mistaken."

There was a shocked silence, broken only by the men on board, Murdo's assistants, who were moving crates. Even the sentry, although he was twenty paces away, seemed frozen with embarrassment.

Murdo's face went white, his eyes, failing to meet Penhaligon's, shifted from side to side. "Must object, sir—no cause for such talk—job to do—hope I know my duty."

"And I know mine, thank God," Penhaligon retorted, "and it includes taking a whip to thieving—"

"Come, Penhaligon," Sir Hubert said, "that's enough. I'm sure you misjudge poor Murdo, although granted that with some assessors and some port admirals your remarks would be justified. You'll get a fair assessment here, I promise you."

"Thank you, sir."

"And you, Murdo, see that this prize is properly valued. Captain Penhaligon is a friend of mine. I wouldn't want to see him cheated."

"Very good, sir." The assessor touched his hat to Sir

Hubert, but his baleful, indignant gaze was on Penhaligon.

"Poor Murdo," Sir Hubert laughed, as they drove away. "He'll never forgive you."

Instead of turning, the carriage continued through the town, up through an area of cultivated fields, to a hillside, yellow with gorse, until on a headland, directly overlooking the sea, it stopped. The coachman got down. "Will this do, sir?"

"Well enough," Sir Hubert replied. "Take yourself off, Jones, for the captain and I have matters to discuss. Be back in half an hour."

They watched the coachman walking, rather self-consciously, along the cliff top, and it was not until he had passed from sight that Sir Hubert spoke.

"Brought you up here, Penhaligon, because it's safe. Too many ears in town, aye, and in my own house I shouldn't wonder. One can't be too careful."

Penhaligon nodded but made no reply. It seemed an extravagant precaution unless Sir Hubert had some extremely personal secret to impart : or perhaps, Penhaligon thought, it was just that he enjoyed the view.

"*Gironde* was crippled, or so I understand—may not even reach port."

"She lost her main yard, sir, and there was other damage, but she must have been holed, more than once, I suspect, below the waterline. *Lyon* reported that as she passed she was low in the water, practically wallowing, but as for reaching port I can't imagine a captain who took her from Aboukir to Barcelona, badly holed and under jury rig, failing to get her the two, three hundred miles she had to go."

Sir Hubert nodded. "You're probably right. Pumping night and day, with improvised fothers. Lamartin isn't the man to give up."

"Nor am I, sir, and with your permission, as soon as we've stepped a new mizzen I'd like to go after him."

"Very well. That's what you were sent for." He hesitated,

while Penhaligon, caught by the beauty of the day and exhilarated by his own happiness, looked out across the blue of sea and sky and thought of Clarissa—Clarissa with his shirt slipping from her shoulders, Clarissa teasing, Clarissa laughing, Clarissa naked in his arms.

"Beg pardon, sir, I was thinking." He felt himself blushing and hoped that Sir Hubert could not read his thoughts.

"I was just saying that I'm worried, desperately worried, about security."

"In what way, sir? With Minorca in our hands, the British fleet in these waters, the French aren't likely to attack."

"That's not what I meant. Intelligence, Penhaligon, that's what worries me. Why is enemy intelligence so much better than ours?"

The old man was serious and clearly troubled, and Penhaligon remembered all the tales he had heard of French and Spanish ships or convoys which had been reported in one sea area and on a certain course mysteriously disappearing and then, a few weeks later, turning up, according to our own tardy intelligence, safe and sound in some other port. *Gironde* was a good example. For more than a year British ships, including at one time a ship of the line with escorting frigates, had been hunting her and yet had not sighted her, even hull down, until *Avenger* found her, or was found by her, a few days ago.

"I don't know, sir, but I can tell you that when we challenged *Lyon* a few days back she responded at once and with the correct signal."

"Devil take it! How could she? You know how long that code has been in force—two, three weeks—yet she knew it."

"What is the answer, sir? Are there spies?"

"There must be."

"Here, in Mahon?"

Sir Hubert hesitated before making a gesture of defeat. "I don't know. I hate to admit it, but I think there must be."

"Among the islanders?"

"I don't know. God knows I have thought about it enough, but I just don't know—how they get their information, how they transmit it. You'd think it was impossible from an island."

"It can only be by sea."

"Or by carrier pigeon. Had you thought of that?"

Penhaligon thought of it now and shook his head. "No, sir. The distance is too great. Besides, the pigeons would have to be brought here, housed and fed : it would be difficult if not impossible to keep the secret."

Sir Hubert agreed, although grudgingly. "You're probably right. So that leaves the sea."

"Neutral vessels, sir : how many come into Mahon?"

"Few enough in all conscience. There aren't many foreigners anxious to get mixed up in our affairs."

"Algerines?"

"Not here. You see their lateen sails in these waters, but only occasionally. They prefer to lie off Barbary."

"So? What else?"

Sir Hubert shrugged. "Greeks and Turks. There's a caique does a round voyage once a month : Gibraltar, Mahon, Valletta, Nicosia."

"What does she carry?"

"Fruit, vegetables, wine, passengers too, although anyone willing to risk his life on such a cockleshell must be insane."

"She might be worth watching, sir."

"With what object? She's neutral. We can't stop and search her. Unless we actually catch her passing information, there's nothing we can do."

"Except see that she doesn't get the information in the first place."

He had said the wrong thing at the wrong moment. He realised that as he saw the colour mounting in Sir Hubert's cheeks and the look of pain and annoyance as he moved his foot. "Damme, sir, do you think I don't know that? D'ye think I'm not doing everything possible?"

"I'm sure you are, sir," Penhaligon said, evenly, "but without success."

Sir Hubert's face was purple. "By God, Penhaligon, you're a plain speaker."

"So are you, sir, with respect, so at least we understand each other."

He knew he was taking a risk, that Sir Hubert would either explode or, if he had any of his daughter's sense of humour, relax. There was no middle course.

To his relief, Sir Hubert subsided. "You're right, Penhaligon, and I'm glad you've come. Somehow we've got to get to the bottom of this. It's imperative that we find how information is leaking. I'm counting on your support."

"Of course, sir, but I have my orders. *Gironde* is my target. I'm only here for a few days."

"That may be enough. You're a clever fellow, Penhaligon, or so I'm told, and you're not—" The old man hesitated.

"A gentleman, sir : is that what you were going to say?"

"Not at all, not at all!" Sir Hubert was embarrassed. "You're not too squeamish : that's all I meant. This is a nasty business and a great deal is at stake. It won't do to fight with kid gloves, Penhaligon—you know that. Someone is leaking information which threatens our every presence in these waters. Someone who's not afraid to play his game must stop him."

NINE

THE next few days were some of the busiest and most happy of his life. From dawn, when he went ashore to harass the dock workers and chandlers, the carpenters, blacksmiths, sail-makers and port officials, to the time, soon after dusk, when he arrived, still full of energy, at the house on Gallows Hill he was busy. Slowly, too slowly by far by his impatient standards, *Avenger*'s scars were healed. Holes were plugged and caulked, a new forward rail fitted, standing rigging was inspected and, where necessary, required. After an interminable delay the mizzen mast was stepped.

He went up to the house on the evening of the third day to report to Sir Hubert and to say goodbye. *Avenger* was ready for sea.

He found Sir Hubert in his study, and as they sat over a glass of Madeira he explained what he had done.

"I have tried to trace the procedure for sailing orders, sir, to see where there could possibly be a leak. As I understand it, they go from you to your secretary, then sometimes, although this is unusual, to the superintendent of the victualling yard."

"Yes. Macpherson is a discreet enough man, not exactly a talker, and sometimes it's necessary."

"Even so, sir, it would be better to cut him out—if that is possible."

"It's possible, but I don't see—"

"This is important, sir: you said so yourself. There's a weak link somewhere and you've asked me to find it."

"Very well."

"Then there's Murdo, sir. I understand he sometimes knows your plans."

Sir Hubert went red, considered a show of anger and decided against it. "Yes, but only occasionally. It's through the captains of outgoing vessels that he sells most of the prizes. He's another one I'd trust."

"Nevertheless, sir, it would be better if he were not informed."

"As you wish."

Penhaligon hesitated. Through the open window he could see the garden and a summer house where Clarissa was talking with Carew. Jealousy? He couldn't believe it was that, yet he found it hard to describe in any other terms the irritation and unease he felt. She was laughing now, perhaps teasing, and to show that there was no unkindness laid her fingers on Carew's arm.

"Beg pardon, sir?"

"I was asking if you had reached any other conclusions."

"Not conclusions, sir, although there are still some enquiries I must make next time I am in Mahon."

"What enquiries?"

"There's one ship, sir, you didn't mention, a Swedish merchantman, a ketch named *Heldstrom*."

"The lemon packet: that's what she's called. I don't think you'd have much satisfaction there."

"Perhaps not, sir, but she's a neutral, so free from search, and, as I understand it, she sails back and forth to Cartagena."

"With lemons. She's been doing it for years. The captain is a Swede who settled here in the eighties."

"I still think, sir, she would bear watching." He didn't say that he had done a fair amount of watching himself, that he had seen Murdo go aboard—furtively, it had seemed—and, perhaps less surprisingly, his own crew member, Larsen. He also remembered that in earlier abortive attempts to find *Gironde*, *Avenger*, presumably with Larsen aboard, had been one of the supporting frigates.

"Well, ye've not been idle, Penhaligon : I see that and I'm grateful. I'll be more grateful still if you track down the spy." Sir Hubert drank his wine and struggled to stand. "Now I expect you'll want to say goodbye to Clarissa."

"Yes, sir." Penhaligon took the old man's arm and helped him to his feet. "There's one thing that puzzles me, sir, something, if you'll forgive me saying so, about which you have been less than frank."

"What? God bless my soul!"

"It's about Jamie, sir. I don't think you have told me the truth."

"Damme, Penhaligon, now you've upset me !" The old man sank back into the chair. "What about Jamie? What don't you believe?"

"You told me, sir, that he had left the Navy, which in itself seems incredible."

"Incredible or not, it's true. Do you want to see the letter from the Admiralty?"

"It's not necessary, sir, for I don't doubt that you would have thought of that."

"Good God, Penhaligon, but you're impertinent !"

"I don't believe Jamie would leave the Navy voluntarily any more than I believe that he could have developed a sudden interest in botany."

"Why not? It's a perfectly respectable pursuit."

"I don't doubt it, sir, but not for Jamie." Penhaligon smiled. "You forget, sir, that we were shipmates together, we shared the same wardroom, sometimes the same watch. You may be able to persuade other people that with England at war Jamie suddenly decided to turn against the sea and to devote his energies to flowers—but not me, sir. I don't believe it."

Sir Hubert was silent for a long time. He sat hunched in his chair, looking old and tired, and his eyes as he turned to Penhaligon were pleading.

"You are right. I should have known you would guess. But

if you have any regard for Jamie you will keep your doubts to yourself."

"Of course."

"Jamie is a linguist, you probably know that. His mother, God bless her, was Spanish and he can speak her lingo, aye and French, like a native."

"So that's what he is doing: he's a British agent?"

"France and Spain, he's visited them both, but more frequently Spain. Whitehall knows and Lethbridge at the Admiralty, but no one else."

"Not even Clarissa?"

"Not even Clarissa."

Penhaligon nodded. "I might have guessed. It's just the thing he'd elect to do." He remembered Jamie in battle, leading a cutting out expedition from *Hyperion*, taking over the quarterdeck when Allison was killed. "He's got courage," he said, "he always had: he'll need all of it on this job."

Sir Hubert nodded. "He'll be shot, of course, if he's caught: he knows that. Yes, he's a brave boy."

"Where does he report, sir, when he's gathered his information?"

"It depends—sometimes Gibraltar, sometimes here, whichever is convenient."

"So that's another reason why we should find this spy—he could betray Jamie?"

"That's about it."

Penhaligon nodded. "Very well, sir. Thank you for telling me. I'd do anything to help Jamie."

The old man nodded gratefully and, once again, struggled to his feet. "Next time he comes—God knows when that will be—I'll tell him I've seen you."

"Thank you, sir, and if you would give him my good wishes."

"Of course." Sir Hubert stopped and, still leaning on Penhaligon's arm, said, "Then I'll wish you God-speed."

96

"Thank you, sir. Now if you will excuse me I must say goodbye to Clarissa."

"Yes." The old man walked with him across the room and stopped at the door. "One thing, Penhaligon—hope you'll forgive me for saying it." He hesitated and cleared his throat. "You have, as you probably know, something of a reputation, a reputation with women."

Penhaligon waited.

"What you've done in the past is no concern of mine. We've all been young once, and wild. But Clarissa is my daughter. I love her very much. I couldn't bear to see her hurt."

Penhaligon took his hand. "Nor I, sir. Whatever my reputation—and I'm sorry if you've heard ill of me—I can only give you my word, sir, that I, too, love her very much. She won't be hurt because of me."

As he went across the lawn, looking towards the summer house where Clarissa and Carew were still talking, he sensed, rather than saw, a movement to his right. The study, which he had just left, abutted on the lawn and was shaded on its western side by a mass of bougainvillea. Something, someone, was there in the shadows, a cat possibly or one of the spaniels of which Clarissa was so fond, and yet his impression, brief as it was, had been of something more furtive.

"Who's there?"

He walked carefully in the half-light to the corner of the house and, even before he reached the flowering bush, he saw a figure moving swiftly across the lawn.

"Stop!"

He hastened his step and, since the figure was moving even more quickly, began to run.

Away from the house, darkness enclosed him so that for a time he was running blind, sinking ankle deep in flower beds, jumping, as he saw the reflected water, across a pond. Ahead, the fugitive was crashing through the undergrowth and, as Penhaligon cleared the bushes, was scaling the wall.

"Stop!"

The man—for he could see enough of the shadow to discern a cloak and a billycock hat—straddled the wall for a moment and then, after quickly glancing to left and right, dropped into the road beyond. When Penhaligon, following suit, reached the top of the wall the man had gone.

Excited by the chase and the thought that the marauder might well have some connection with Sir Hubert's spy, he forgot Clarissa, at least until he was some way from the house, and by that time it was too late. He was already approaching the outskirts of town.

Two seamen sat outside an inn, one, a topman whose name he had forgotten, more than half seas over, the other, the ubiquitous Larsen, sober. He stopped beside them and made an impatient movement with his hand as they struggled to rise.

"A man came down this road a few minutes ago. Did you see him?"

"No, sir." The drunken man was having difficulty in remaining upright : even as he spoke his elbow slipped from the table. "Didn't see nothing."

"What about you, Larsen?"

"Maybe, sir—I think so."

"When was this?"

"Two, three minutes ago. I was just coming out with a glass."

"Did you get a look at him?"

"No, sir. He wasn't a seaman, if that's what you mean."

"I know that, but had you seen him before? Would you recognise him again?"

"No, sir—sorry, sir."

He continued down the hill, but with a realisation as he entered the maze of streets that his quarry had slipped away. Men and women in family groups were sitting in their patios or, in the poorer quarter, outside in the streets. Children were playing, cats and dogs were sniffing among the garbage : there was a smell of wood smoke and ordure and sweet-scented flowers. It was a relief to come out on the quayside and catch the smell of the sea.

"Good evening, Mr Murdo."

The assessor, looking even more smug in his buckled shoes, silk stockings, breeches, cut-away jacket and billycock hat, was arm in arm with an equally respectable-looking lady of middle age.

"Good evening, sir." Murdo's greeting was stiff and un-friendly. "May I present my wife?"

Penhaligon doffed his hat and bowed and, as he straightened, looked as closely as he dared at Murdo's waist-coat. Was there a smudge of dirt there, a trace of lichen that might have rubbed off from the top of a wall? He couldn't be certain. "Your servant, ma'am."

"Mrs Murdo and I are taking the air," the assessor said. "That is why we are so late. My wife finds the heat of the day excessive."

"I agree with you, ma'am," Penhaligon said. "I count myself fortunate to spend most of my time in the cooler air at sea."

As he left them and retraced his steps up the hill, he wondered whether Murdo, that fat, pompous creature, could possibly have the agility, or indeed the nerve, to trespass on Sir Hubert's property or, on being discovered, would scale a wall.

It was a warm, dry evening with only a light breeze which, he hoped, would strengthen by morning; the dusty road and the flanking bushes of gorse and bougainvillea showed clearly in the darkness : in the deeper shadows of a tree two lovers were locked in a timeless embrace. He stopped as he heard someone coming down the road.

"You're too late, sir," Carew said. "Miss Clarissa has gone to bed."

"Already? It's only nine o'clock."

"I think, sir, she had a headache."

Penhaligon continued up the hill, ignoring Carew's following cry, "It's too late, sir. She asked me to say goodbye."

Damn and blast the man! He was angry now, no, more than angry, he was jealous. The fact that Carew, rather than himself, had spent this last evening in Clarissa's company was none of his fault. Or was it? For the first time in any love affair, he was concerned that he should not be misunderstood.

As he went in by the main gate and, leaving the drive, set off across the lawn, he looked up at the window of Clarissa's bedroom. At first it was in darkness, but even as he walked a light appeared and in a moment Clarissa, still fully dressed, came to the balcony.

He ran forward.

"Clarissa!"

She looked down and, with just a hint of laughter in her voice, called, "Who's there?"

"Napoleon Bonaparte. I've taken over the island."

"Again? Really, this is getting rather tiresome."

"Don't trifle with me, madam, just come outside to the lawn."

"I don't know." She looked at him demurely. "Perhaps I'm safer here."

"You'll never be safe from me, ma'am, not while you insist on making yourself so adorable."

"Oh, Cocky!" She giggled and blew him a kiss. "One moment, your majesty, I'm coming."

TEN

LIKE a wolf in the fold, *Avenger* prowled the sea plains of Valencia, from Tortosa Point to Cap de la Nao, lurking near or just beyond the horizon, coming in on the trade and swooping with killing speed and efficiency every time a Spanish sail appeared. In a month they took five merchantmen and sent another ashore; the Spanish fleet, such as it was, made half-hearted attempts to engage her, without ever venturing far from land, and Spanish crews refused to leave their shallow coastal waters. The legend of the "English Captain" grew. From the crew of one prize they learnt that *Gironde* was in dock in Barcelona. The captain, who had no reason to love the French, reported that she was on her side, with gaping holes in her hull, and that it would be weeks, if not months, before she could put to sea again. *Avenger* continued her patrol.

South of Alicante they found more shipping, yawls, ketches, schooners, and a brigantine which, on being challenged, was promptly scuttled. There were lateen-sailed Arab vessels, too, and, as they approached the Atlantic, an increasing number of ships carrying neutral flags. Returning—for Penhaligon could not risk sailing too far from Barcelona—they saw *Heldstrom* running before the wind, her jib sails curving gracefully and driver billowing as she plunged across the bay.

"She'll make good speed to Cartagena," McNeil observed.

"Yes. I'd give a hundred guineas to board her," Penhaligon replied, "to search her cargo and, even more, the captain's cabin. I wonder what treacherous information we'd find."

"You think that this is the way information is smuggled abroad?" McNeil asked.

"It's one way, although I doubt that we'll ever prove it."

"Unfortunately we can't afford to molest her," McNeil reminded. "We'd have the government at home after our blood if we upset Sweden."

It was quite true. With most of Europe in arms, the few uncommitted nations watched from the sides-lines, weighing Napoleon's land victories against the sea power of the British, and unable to guess at this stage, or so they thought, the final victor. In the meantime they remained vociferously neutral.

McNeil cleared his throat, a habit he had whenever he was about to announce bad news. "If I may remind you, sir, we shall have to make land soon, for the water is running low and some of the salt beef is uneatable."

Penhaligon nodded. "I know. I'm almost tempted to set course for Mahon, if only to confront that damned victualling superintendent."

"They're all rogues, sir," McNeil replied, echoing the generally accepted view of the time.

"The trouble is," Penhaligon continued, "I begrudge the time. It would be unforgivable if *Gironde* came out while we're away."

"It's a risk, sir, but, if I may say so, a small one. If the information we have is correct, it will be some weeks yet before she's seaworthy."

"Perhaps you're right."

"There's another point, sir; even if we had enough fresh food and water, we are still desperately short of crew. If it came to a full-scale engagement we'd be hard put to manoeuvre."

Penhaligon did not reply, although he knew that McNeil was right. It was something that had been worrying him for a long time. Depleted by prize crews, which included the two junior officers, Meldrum and Hardcastle, two of the midshipmen and the senior boatswain's mate, *Avenger* was dangerously undermanned. And yet in his fierce determination to sink

Gironde he found it hard to accept the common sense view that he should return to port.

"We'll see," he said. "Unless we're engaged beforehand, we'll sail north to Barcelona. If there's no sight of *Gironde* we'll make for Mahon."

McNeil smiled and nodded, perhaps realising that from this aggressive captain it was a more generous concession than he had any right to expect.

He said, "Unless the wind changes we'll be off Barcelona some time tomorrow and we can be in Mahon by Wednesday."

Penhaligon looked aloft to the great spread of canvas arched against the sky as *Avenger* clawed her way northwards. Pitch and roll, pitch and roll; the steady movement as the bows met the sea and the sound of wind in the rigging were as comforting as a cradle song. He was proud of his ship and even more proud of his men, who, in the manner of British seamen, had responded to discipline and were, he would swear, as anxious to meet *Gironde* as he was. Through his glass he saw the measureless expanse of blue ahead and, to larboard, the Spanish coastline near Valencia, some ten miles distant. These coastal waters, which in times of peace would have been full of shipping, were empty. The only sail in view was *Heldstrom.*

It was chance or perhaps no more than idle curiosity which made him train his glass on the Swedish vessel. She was still in view, hull up, which surprised him, for with all sail set and the wind on her quarter she had been making all of six knots.

"What do you make of that?" He passed the glass to McNeil.

"That's strange, sir. She's taking in canvas."

"She's also altering course."

"So she is. But why?"

"Why, indeed!" He put the glass to his eye again in time to see *Heldstrom* disappearing behind a headland. He beckoned to the midshipman of the watch. "Pass word for Mr Lubbock." He said to McNeil, "There are questions I would like to ask. Why, for instance, is she in these waters at all? If she's making for Cartagena she would have been better advised to take the direct course east of Mallorca."

"You're right, sir. And even if she chose to go west, her course shouldn't take her so close to land. She'll still have to clear Cap de la Nao."

"You wanted me, sir?" Lubbock, the master, had been plotting their course in the chart room.

"Yes, Mr Lubbock. I want you to take a bearing on that point yonder. Tell me what lies beyond."

"Aye, aye, sir."

"In the meantime, Mr McNeil, I'll trouble you to take in head sails. I'm tempted to take a look."

"Aye, aye, sir." If McNeil was dismayed by the prospect of further delay, he was too loyal to show it. "Hands to reduce canvas!"

It took Lubbock, who was deliberate in all his actions but made up for it by being accurate, all of ten minutes to take a bearing, consult chart and announce in a tone of certainty that they were looking at Cullera Point. "There's Valencia, sir, on our larboard bow; that's Albufera abeam."

"Thank you, Mr Lubbock. And what lies beyond?"

"The town, sir—Cullera, in the deep set of the bay."

"Thank you." Penhaligon turned to McNeil. "We'll take a look, Mr McNeil. Change course, if you please."

"Stand by for change of course! Stand by!"

As *Avenger* turned before the wind the crew, who sensed a measure of excitement after hours of monotonous tacking, hauled enthusiastically at sheets and braces and then steadied themselves against the bulwark as the deck tilted and the sea rose above the tumble-home on the larboard beam.

"How long to sunset, Mr McNeil?"

"Two hours, sir; two hours and twelve minutes to be precise."

It was unfortunate, Penhaligon thought, that he had not taken his decision earlier, although he was comforted by the thought that if he had there would have been no chance of concealing his intention from *Heldstrom*, which was now out of sight, somewhere beyond Cullera Point. *Avenger* could approach with the wind on her quarter and, so he hoped, in secret.

"What course, sir?" McNeil asked.

"Steady as she goes. We'll go in as close as we dare, north of the point, and then see how the coast lies. Send a look-out to the fore topgallant masthead, if you please."

"Aye, aye, sir."

"And, Mr McNeil. Have a man with a lead standing by at the main chains."

These were dangerous waters off this Spanish coast, with gently shelving bottoms and sandy beaches, so that it was easy, as many an unfortunate captain had found, to run aground.

The point was near now; he could see the beach and a low cliff, surmounted by palms, and, further inland, some olive groves. On the point, overlooking the sea, although almost completely surrounded by flowering bushes and trees, was a castle.

"It looks quiet enough," McNeil observed.

"Yes, although it's not the Spanish I'm concerned with." Like all captains, he had a horror of lee shores.

"Well, sir, it looks safe enough. There's nothing to the horizon."

"Only we don't know what's beyond the point."

Their attention was caught by a cry from the leadsman in the chains. "No bottom with this line, sir."

Penhaligon nodded. That meant at least twenty fathoms. Canvas had been reduced to topsails and topgallants and, coming within the shelter of land, *Avenger* was reduced to three knots. He watched the man in the chains swing and then heave his lead. The weight, attached to a rope marked with stripes and leather and pieces of red, white and blue cloth and with a splicing of yarn at the twenty-fathom mark, curved in the air and fell with a gentle splash into the sea ahead.

They waited as the leadsman coiled in the slack and, when it passed vertically below, they heard him call, "By the deep eighteen." There was still plenty of depth, although the shore with its curve of sand and its upturned fishing boats and a fringe of palms seemed uncomfortably near.

"By the mark ten."

They were shoaling fast. He was conscious of McNeil and Lubbock watching anxiously.

"And a half seven."

That was close enough. "Heave to, Mr McNeil, if you please."

Spain, on closer acquaintance, seemed a pleasant enough place. With shadows lengthening in the evening sun, trees, bushes and even the few rocks on the beach were sharply delineated. On the headland a mass of scarlet blossom marked what must have been the seaward boundary of the castle grounds, while directly ahead, where a fisherman's cottage, hardly more than a shack, nestled in the trees a hedge of bougainvillea ringed the beach.

"Lower away the longboat! Crew armed with cutlasses, Mr Simmons, if you please. Ask Mr Dexter to send two of his marines."

He couldn't believe that they would meet any opposition in what appeared to be a particularly remote and sparsely populated area, but he couldn't afford to take chances. He still had no way of knowing what lay beyond the point.

As he took his position in the stern-sheets he looked up at *Avenger* towering above, the pitch on her hull rough and blistered from this angle and the plugging of holes made by *Gironde*'s shot clearly visible : by the taffrail McNeil looked down with anxious face.

"Give way."

With oars dipping in unison and the coxswain at the tiller steering a close course, the longboat moved round the headland, past a small cove and a beach with a yacht at anchor, until it emerged suddenly in the wide expanse of the bay.

There were mountains beyond, and, nearer, perhaps a mile distant, the white houses and red-roofed cottages of Cullera. There were boats and a few larger vessels, all huddled together, in the harbour—it was difficult to see them clearly in the fading light—and, at anchor, half a mile from shore, a Spanish ship of the line.

El Cid: he knew at once that it was her from the curious cut of her prow and the rather clumsy line of her sheer. She was lying at anchor, with yards lowered, despite the fact that *Avenger* must have passed on the horizon only an hour since.

Nearer, only a hundred yards away, lay the ketch *Heldstrom*.

She was anchored perhaps a cable's length from shore, beside what appeared to be a deserted beach. There was no sign of activity on her deck and only a beached dinghy to show that anyone had gone ashore. Inland there was nothing that he could see apart from some orchards—of lemons?—and a donkey track up the hill.

"Take her in, Mr Simmons. I'm going to have a look."

He was taking a chance, he knew, for if *El Cid* was fully manned and became aware of *Avenger*'s presence she could make canvas and round the point long before he could regain his ship. On the other hand, *Heldstrom* was so near.

There was no one watching from her deck as the longboat glided through the still water and grounded on the beach.

"Have her pulled ashore, Mr Simmons—under cover, if you can. Baghot, come with me."

Feeling slightly ridiculous, for he would be a laughing stock if it was found that the Swedish ship had merely stopped to pick up lemons, he moved under the cover of trees towards the anchored ketch and the dinghy. Close on his heels, Baghot, with a knife in his hand, was following silently, hoping no doubt that they would encounter at least a few Spaniards.

In fact they encountered only one.

As they turned a bend in the path they found themselves in a clearing where the ground had been built up to support a summer house, covered with roses and bougainvillea, with a fine view of the sea. Enjoying the view, until their unexpected appearance, was a young woman.

She rose at once and turned as though to run, but then, as arrogance over-rode fear, she stopped.

"Who are you? What do you want?"

"You speak English?" Penhaligon smiled with all his charm as he came to the foot of the mound and saluted.

"As you see." She was young, and yet not so young that her gown, with its low-cut bosom and elegant draperies, could hide a certain voluptuousness, which was evident, too, in her eyes and her full, red lips. "Are you—? Yes, you must be. Are you the English Captain?"

"Penhaligon, ma'am, at your service."

"Of *Avenger*?"

His smile hardened. "You are well informed."

She shrugged. "I am the Marquesa de Cullera y Alicante. We have good reason to know your name, señor, for we have suffered much from your piracy."

"We are at war, ma'am, your country and mine: this is no piracy, but a blockade."

"Call it what you will, the result is the same. The crops are grown but not gathered, the fruit rots on the trees. We, my husband and I, grow poorer while the peasants starve."

Penhaligon pointed through the trees to *Heldstrom*, which still lay silent, without any visible crew, a short distance from shore. "Not all your fruit rots on the trees, apparently."

"*Heldstrom*! A hundred-ton ketch! Do you know what proportion of our crops she can carry?"

"At least she comes—and she is neutral."

"Yes. Would that there were more like her, but you know what happens? The blood of every neutral turns to water when he hears talk of the British Navy."

"How often does she come?"

"Once or twice a month. She is still trying to clear last season's crop." She looked at him with growing surprise. "Is that why you came ashore—to investigate the lemon packet?"

Penhaligon did not reply.

"You must be mad. Didn't you know she was neutral? Was it for her you put your head into a noose?"

"I'm not aware, ma'am, that my head is in a noose—unless you propose to shoot us down from your battlements as we round the point."

She shook her head. "Simpler than that, although your suggestion is not without merit. You see, señor, I have only to walk a short distance to my home—you saw the castle on the headland?—and tell my servant, who was until recently a seaman on *San Josef*, to signal across the bay, and *El Cid* will make sail and put to sea long before you and your men can return to *Avenger*."

Penhaligon looked at her admiringly. She was a fine figure of a woman, and if he had not been in love with Clarissa he would have done his best to charm her. But there was no time. She was quite right when he said that *El Cid* posed a threat. Although darkness was falling, there would still be time, if the signal were given now, for her to make sail, round the headland and engage *Avenger* before he could return. *Avenger*, he remembered only too well, was on a lee shore.

"You are right, ma'am. I take your point. So, since I have no intention of allowing my ship to be taken unawares, there is only one thing I can do. I must, regretfully, make you my prisoner."

ELEVEN

HE RAN up the mound so quickly that, even if she had been so minded, she would have had no chance to escape. The path to the castle must have lain behind the summer house, for she was clearly not used to descending the steep, grass-covered slope to the lower path—it was no more than a track—where Baghot was waiting. Guided by Penhaligon's arm, she slid and ran to the lower level and then, incredulous more than angry, made her stand.

"You wouldn't dare!"

"Alas, yes, ma'am," Penhaligon said. "Necessity is no gentleman."

"Nor you, sir, it appears."

"You will be taken aboard, treated with every respect, I need hardly add, and put ashore again as soon as we are free of *El Cid*."

She laughed. "So you are afraid. You are not, as some of my compatriots believe, invincible."

"Not invincible, ma'am, nor yet afraid—" he looked at her narrowly, "although since I doubt you'll accept my word I'm tempted to prove it."

"Engage *El Cid*?"

"Perhaps."

She laughed even more scornfully, and said again, "You wouldn't dare!"

It was dusk before they reached the longboat. Simmons, the twelve oarsmen and the two red-jackets emerged silently from the bushes and, with only a signal from the captain, began to slide the heavy boat into the water. The sun was sinking across the bay and the town, too distant now to be seen in detail, the Spanish ship of war and the still, almost waveless, sea were red. Firmly holding the marquesa's arm, Penhaligon followed the longboat across the beach. The oarsmen were abroad, the marines followed and took their places in the bows : only the coxswain remained, steadying the boat by the stern.

"Do you really want to take me aboard?" the marquesa asked.

"I'm afraid so."

"I could scream. You realise that? Someone would hear."

"Then, regretfully, I should be forced to silence you." He didn't explain how and she thought better than to ask as she allowed him to help her into the boat.

"Give way."

Pulled by twelve oars, which dipped as one into a blood-red sea, the longboat moved silently towards the point. It was almost dark. The headland, with the flaming bushes, the line of palm trees and the castellated walls of the castle beyond showed in outline only, and as they cleared the farthest cliff *Avenger* appeared as a ghostly ship riding a silent sea.

"Shall I make sail, sir?" If McNeil was surprised to see the marquesa he was too polite or perhaps had too much respect for his captain to show it.

"If you please, Mr McNeil. Let us get away from this lee shore." He turned to the marquesa, who was watching him from the darkness, and said. "I must ask you to go below, ma'am, and to accept the hospitality of my cabin." He saw her expression and added, "I will have my things removed. You have nothing to fear."

She made no reply, but turned and followed Baghot down the companion.

"Sleep well, ma'am," Penhaligon called after her. "You will be ashore again before morning."

Even as he said it, he wondered if it were true. The safest and indeed the obvious course, remembering their depleted

111

condition, would be to put out to sea while the Spanish ship of war was still unaware of their presence, and at dawn, provided they had not been pursued, to lower away the gig and have the marquesa put ashore. That was the safe course.

Yet, standing on the quarterdeck as *Avenger* turned her bows to the wind and seeing the lights of Cullera diminishing until they were mere pin-pricks against the darkness, he thought of *El Cid*, that big, ungainly ship of war and her curious air of unpreparedness as she rode at anchor, half a mile from shore.

He wondered whether there were batteries at Cullera. It seemed unlikely. From recent skirmishes along this coast it had seemed that the Spanish, perhaps because they were reluctant allies, were generally indifferent fighters and, more often than not, unprepared. As the lights of Cullera finally disappeared he made up his mind.

"Call hands, Mr Carew, if you please. Prepare to change course."

None of the crew on *Avenger* would forget that night. As the ship turned once again before the wind and made for the Spanish coast they knew that before morning they would be engaged in combat.

In the wardroom, with an admiralty chart on the table, Penhaligon explained his intention.

"*El Cid* lies in Cullera Bay," he said. "We, and I mean every officer and man we can muster, are going to fetch her out."

He watched their reactions carefully, Carew incredulous, Lubbock dismayed, McNeil firmly non-committal. Only Dexter of the marines and Lovegrove seemed glad, while Keegan, who as the only remaining midshipman realised that he would certainly be involved, nervously licked his lips but managed a smile.

"A cutting out expedition, sir?" McNeil asked.

"Yes. I know it sounds hazardous, but no more so than other missions we've undertaken : and I believe we can do it."

The English Captain

"But, sir," Carew said, "she's a ship of the line."

"I'm aware of that."

"And we are understrength, embarrassingly so: we'd be hard put to manoeuvre the ship in battle."

"We are not going to manoeuvre ship, Mr Carew. We are going to run in before the wind, heave-to to windward of Cullera Point." He paused as he saw Lubbock's expression. "Oh, don't worry. We'll leave you sea way. At four-twenty, an hour before dawn, Mr Carew in the cutter, Mr Lovegrove in the gig and myself in the longboat will make across the bay. Our intention will be to take *El Cid* by surprise. The watch below will be asleep, or so we'll hope, and it's unlikely that the watch on deck will be much better."

"But, sir," Carew argued, "we shall have—what?—eighty men!"

"Ninety. Mr Dexter, I'll want all your marines. They'll have to squeeze in as best they can. It won't be comfortable."

"Aye, aye, sir."

Penhaligon looked round the table and smiled. "The odds seem great, gentlemen, but no more than we've accepted before. Our trump cards will be surprise, for from past experience I don't believe the Spaniards will be alert, surprise and determination."

Carew cleared his throat as though to speak and thought better of it; Dexter grinned and rubbed his hands and moved nearer the table; Lubbock looked anxiously at the chart.

"Very well, gentlemen. This is how we will do it."

The night was dark and moonless as the three boats set off across the water. With oars muffled and the faces of officers and crew blackened with lamp soot, it looked like a ghostly cortège, Penhaligon thought, and the mournful cry of a seagull added to the illusion. Lovegrove in the gig was leading, with Carew in the cutter following and Penhaligon in the longboat last. When they sighted *El Cid* the order would be reversed.

It must be soon, Penhaligon thought, looking anxiously seawards where the first streaks of dawn were in the sky. To starboard a few lights fixed the position of Cullera, but they were too distant to threaten danger and any help from that direction could scarcely arrive in time.

"Ship ahead, sir!" He heard the coxswain's whisper as he saw the gig, some twenty yards ahead, rest oars.

He nodded and motioned to the longboat crew to continue. In the last hour of the graveyard watch he had made sure that everyone, from Carew to the most humble waister, knew exactly what he had to do.

As they drew nearer he waited anxiously, scarcely daring to breathe lest he miss some noise or challenge from *El Cid*, which rose above them like a sea monster, her curving prow and blunt stern just visible in the gathering light. Waves were gently lapping her hull. There was no sentry that he could see and, knowing the Spaniard's lax discipline, he imagined him with his mates, sitting against a bulwark or by the forward hatch, swapping yarns or sleeping, while the officer of the watch thought longingly of his bunk.

"Careful!"

The order was unnecessary, for although the rowers could not see the hull behind them the coxswain had already moved forward with a boathook and was crouching in the thwarts.

The vessels came together with scarcely a sound. Simmons was making fast to the main chains while his mate in the cutter steered a course astern. A slow count to sixty was what he had ordered, from the moment the longboat tied up to the time when the crews of both started their assault. The gig, hidden from view of deck by the tumble-home, had a separate role.

"Now!" Helped by Baghot's strong arm, he grasped a chain plate and, as silently as he could manage, clambered towards the deck.

"*Alto!*"

The challenge, an exclamation of surprise, warned him that Carew on the larboard side had reached deck before him. He heard a further challenge and then a shout and, as he swung over the bulwark, the whistle of a shot.

The man who had fired it, a Spanish officer, caught unawares, without his hat or jacket and in stockinged feet, was standing by the taffrail. His face, which was just visible in the growing light, showed utter consternation as he raised the pistol again and pulled the trigger on an empty chamber.

"*Avenger*!" Drawing his sword to rally the men behind him, Penhaligon leapt up the companion and, before the unfortunate officer had time to prime his pistol, Penhaligon had dispatched him with a slash to the throat.

There was another officer, a midshipman, who woke from his doze by the binnacle and, seeing in one glance the almost decapitated body of his companion and the blackened face of his attacker, vented a high-pitched scream and vaulted over the side. Penhaligon was already half-way down the companion before he heard the splash.

"To the fo'c'sle, lads! Baghot and you, Larsen, come with me."

The Spanish captain, more alert than some of his officers, came from his cabin sword in hand, and, although hampered by his jacket, which he had only half donned, immediately challenged.

Penhaligon was an effective rather than a polished swordsman. Action in the narrow passage, dimly lit by a night lamp, was to his advantage, for there was little room to manoeuvre, and as their blades met the Spaniard could hardly have foreseen that following his lunge the English captain would keep coming forward. It was too dark for swordsmanship. Penhaligon leapt at him, trusting to his superior weight to secure the Spaniard's sword arm, and as they embraced, both breathing heavily, he butted his opponent in the face.

The Spaniard fell back, half-blinded and with blood streaming from his nose. He made to speak, to utter some indignant protest, but with the words still unuttered he fell to Penhaligon's sword.

Stepping over his body, Penhaligon came to more cabins, only one of which was occupied, and leaving Baghot to deal with a foppish gentleman still in his night clothes who was staring, bewildered, from his cot, he ran forward, past the main cabin and the wardroom, to the main hatch.

"How's it going, sir?" Simmons, the coxswain, his cutlass arm spattered with blood, met him on the companion.

"I'm not sure. I've accounted for three, no four, officers. There must be more."

"On the maindeck, sir. They're out there now, rallying the crew."

"Very well. You, Mr Simmons, take Baghot and Larsen below. See what's skulking between decks."

"Aye, aye, sir."

As Penhaligon came out on the maindeck he was immediately enveloped in hand-to-hand fighting, and, since he had emerged among the advancing Spaniards, he had no option but to fight his way aft. He dispatched one slow-witted crewman before he could open his mouth, then, beckoning to imaginary Englishmen below, shouted, "Follow me, lads!", and, with a blood-curdling cry, thrust and parried a way through the Spaniards until he reached Carew on the quarterdeck.

"How are we faring?"

"Not badly, sir, but it won't be long, I'm afraid, before numbers will tell."

"We'll win, Mr Carew, never fear. Our lads are holding well and we've still a few tricks in our bag."

One of the tricks was revealed almost immediately, and, in view of the deteriorating situation on deck, not a moment too soon. Lovegrove, who with a few marines and a seaman had been waiting patiently under the bows, suddenly emerged on the fo'c'sle head and, calling to more imaginary comrades below, gave the order to fire. One boatswain and a seaman with cutlasses and pistols and four marines with muskets could hardly be a decisive force against two hundred or more

Spaniards now fighting on deck, but the boatswain's party had the advantage of surprise. They also had behind them the sun which had just cleared the horizon.

"Fire!"

At a distance of twenty yards the Englishmen could hardly miss. The front rank of Spaniards fell, and the rest retreated, confusing their comrades aft, who were already being harassed by Penhaligon and his crew.

For ten minutes or more the Englishmen prospered, taking full advantage of the confusion on deck, and, by repeatedly uttering fiendish cries, managed to instil a quite unjustified fear in the minds of the Spaniards. But, as Carew had said, numbers began to tell. Although the Englishmen were still fighting, they were tired and at times in danger of being overwhelmed, and only the example of Penhaligon himself, whose tall, angular figure was always in the thick of the fray, sustained them.

Then there was another diversion, equally welcome, as Baghot and Larsen appeared.

They emerged from the main hatch and by good fortune at a moment when the tide of battle had passed. They stepped out on to a deck already heavily stained with blood and littered with the prostrate forms of fallen seamen, and saw that the main body of Spaniards was aft, with its backs to them, as it fought to gain a foothold on the quarterdeck. The attack of Baghot and Larsen when it came was from the rear.

On the quarterdeck, locked in combat with a Spanish officer who was not only as ruthless as himself but an excellent swordsman, Penhaligon still had time to see the Englishman and the Swede start their murderous attack.

It was simply but efficiently done. Without fuss or panic they set about the Spaniards, who, thinking that their rear was secure, since Lovegrove and the red-coats had long been forced below, were taken by surprise when a strong arm seized them by shirt or collar, swung them round where another arm, equally strong, dispatched them. Only a torn shirt which enabled a screaming seaman to escape gave the warning, and the survivors, too taken aback or perhaps too afraid to act, made only half-hearted attempts to stop them as they made the quarterdeck.

"Well done, lads!" Penhaligon shouted, and then, as his attention wavered, had his sword whipped from his hand.

"Surrender!" The Spanish officer was pressing him against the taffrail with a sword at his throat.

"For myself, or are you talking about the crew?"

"You first, *capitan*, then you will give orders to the crew."

"Well, I can hardly do that from this position."

Assuming, incorrectly, that this was tantamount to surrender, the Spanish officer relaxed his grasp and, as they straightened, Penhaligon kneed him in the groin.

The Spanish officer doubled up, screaming with pain, and before he could recover Penhaligon seized him by the leg and shoulder and pitched him over the rail.

He came forward and stood beside Baghot, who was fighting fiercely to prevent the Spaniards, still more than a hundred strong, ascending the companion. He grinned as he saw his captain. "Are you all right, sir?"

For the moment, Penhaligon thought, but for how much longer? The Englishmen were very tired now and had suffered many casualties. The Spaniards still outnumbered them five to one. There was one last chance.

"Larsen!" He took the Swede's arm and pulled him from the fray. "The Spanish colours, up there on the masthead—do you think you can get them?"

Larsen smiled and nodded and then lumbered to the shrouds.

It was incredible, Penhaligon thought, that after a long day and an even longer night, after a fight which had now waxed to and fro for more than an hour, the topman could still find energy to clamber up the rigging. He came to the signal yard and with the ease of a child plucking a flower dragged down the Spanish colours and allowed them to flutter to the deck.

Someone—it could have been an Englishman—shouted and pointed upwards. A groan came from the Spaniards, and, bewildered, tired and leaderless, they suddenly lost spirit and surrendered.

TWELVE

"I'LL leave you the marines," Penhaligon said, "in case you have trouble with the crew. You'll need a constant guard, day and night, although I doubt that any will show signs of fight. If they do, shoot them: you have my permission. In fact, it might be a good thing to have a dissenter early on. A dead Spaniard would be a powerful argument."

"With respect, sir," Carew said, "I am a British officer. I know how to behave."

"You're a *live* British officer," Penhaligon retorted. "That's the important thing." He smiled. They were both tired and more than a little dishevelled, and Carew, to his surprise, had fought well. "But you could be right."

"What about *Avenger*, sir," Carew asked. "If I may say so, you have left yourself scarcely a workable crew."

"We shall manage. Watch on, watch off: we should be in Mahon in two days."

"I hope so."

The two Spanish officers still alive had already been escorted to *Avenger*. Carew, with Keegan and the boatswain to share the watch, and ninety members of *Avenger*'s crew had been ordered to sail *El Cid* to Minorca. She was a big, unwieldy vessel, with more nuisance value to the British than any threat as a fighting ship of the line, but she would be a valuable prize.

"Well, I'll leave you in charge."

"Sail ho! Sail dead ahead!"

Penhaligon looked up sharply, in consternation but also

120

with a glow of satisfaction that almost the first thing he had
ordered after the surrender was a look-out.

"Masthead! What do you see?"

"Two sail, sir, hull down. Could be frigates."

Damn! He beat his fist into the palm of his hand. If they
were frigates they were almost certainly Spanish—or French:
with scarcely enough crew to man one ship, let alone two, he
was in no position to fight.

"Hadn't we better transfer back to *Avenger*, sir?" Carew
asked. "At least we could escape."

It was a sensible, even a realistic suggestion: no court of
enquiry would condemn him for ensuring the safety of his
ship, even if it meant deserting the prize. But he knew,
stubbornly, that he would never do that: if necessary he
would burn her.

Then he remembered a ruse which British and French had
played on one another when the odds were against them.
Perhaps the Spanish knew of it, too.

"Mr Keegan!" he called. "See what flags they have in the
signal locker."

"Sir?"

"See if you can find a Jack."

He waited, hands clasped behind his back, ignoring Carew's
pursed lips and look of spinsterish disapproval. It was a
chance, and if, as seemed likely, they proved to be French
ships of war, it might work.

"Yes, sir!" Keegan came running aft with a large Union
flag trailing behind him.

"Good!" He turned to Carew. "There you are, then. That's
what we'll do. Run up the Jack, which even you can do with
a clear conscience since the ship is in our hands. We'll go
out and meet 'em, *El Cid* as a British ship of the line, *Avenger*
as her escort."

"But, sir—!"

"No 'buts', Mr Carew. Those are my orders."

Under all plain sail, *Avenger* and *El Cid* plunged eastwards

121

with the wind on their bows, their decks cleared, with guns run out and, as an extra precaution, side nettings fixed to repel boarders. Penhaligon prayed fervently that they would not have to engage. Even one frigate, or an efficiently captained sloop of war, for that matter, would be too much for them in these conditions. *Avenger* had scarcely enough men to handle braces and take in canvas, while Carew on *El Cid*, although numerically more fortunate, had the worries of a strange ship and a proportion of hostile crew.

"So, captain, your word is as unacceptable as your manners."

"Marquesa!" He looked at her with consternation, for, literally, until that moment she had never entered his mind. "My deepest apologies, ma'am, but I forgot you."

"Hm! Not the most charming way to tell me, perhaps, but at least you are honest."

"No." He took her hand, wanting her to understand. "I meant to put you ashore. I promised. But circumstances have changed. Out there are two enemy ships of war."

"And you are going to engage them?"

"It's all I can do."

She smiled and shook her head. "Now I know what they mean when they talk of the 'English Captain'." She turned and leant on the rail. "You must be mad!"

"Not mad, just determined." He leant on the taffrail beside her and saw that in profile she was beautiful, with dark eyes fanned by long lashes, a straight nose and full red lips. She turned as she sensed his scrutiny and with the air of a woman who knows her own beauty calmly met his gaze.

"So, you will have to take me to Mahon—is that it?"

"I'm afraid so. I'll bring you back as soon as I can."

"If the French don't capture you first." She nodded towards the horizon where the two frigates could just be seen.

"How do you know they are French?"

She shrugged. "Perhaps I have better eyesight than you."

122

"Perhaps." He said, "At worst, you could travel back on *Heldstrom.*"

"It wouldn't be the first time."

"What?" He stared at her in surprise. "You mean you've been aboard her?"

"Of course."

"Where to?"

"Cartagena, Port Mahon."

"You've been to Mahon?"

"Why not? We haven't always been at war."

"Of course not." He knew that he was tired and that he probably sounded stupid, but he found her answers confusing.

She said, "There are a number of things about me that will surprise you, captain."

"What do you mean?"

"No matter." She shook her head and made to return to the cabin. "After the battle—if you are still free."

"Very well." He called after her, "Marquesa!"

She didn't even break her step. "I know. The bulkheads are down, so you want me in the cable tier."

With the wind on their quarter, the enemy ships were approaching fast. They were frigates, French, for through his glass he could see the hated tricolour, and probably out of Toulon, which since Hood's withdrawal seven years earlier had been the major base for French incursions into the Mediterranean.

"Prepare to go about!"

On the new tack, *Avenger* would be making directly towards them, a natural manoeuvre if she were the scouting frigate for the more ponderous ship of the line. At least, he thought, the French captains could hardly mistake *Avenger* for anything but British. And, even if they recognised, or thought they recognised, *El Cid* as Spanish, they would be confused: better still, he thought, coming from Toulon and with no great respect for their Spanish ally, they might never have seen *El Cid*.

"Still coming, sir," McNeil observed.

Penhaligon nodded and stood with feet astride, against the swaying deck, and his hands tightly clasped behind his back, the customary pose he adopted when he was under strain. *El Cid* with her reluctant crew, egged on by the watchful marines, was following on the new tack.

He hoped that the French would not notice anything unusual. The big ship of the line was always more difficult to sail into the wind or at least could never manoeuvre as quickly or as smartly as her attendant frigates, and, to give him credit, Carew was managing pretty well. As *El Cid* came round into the wind her foreyards were braced, then as she came still further and the wind caught her on the new tack, main and mizzen yards followed suit.

He remembered the same desperate tactic he had used in his encounter with *Gironde*, although the conditions then had been very different, and wondered, although he had not suggested as much to Sir Hubert, whether this had not been at least partly responsible for the subsequent loss of his mizzen. Luck, as he had always known, was often the difference between failure and success, and he knew that he was lucky. The mast could have gone earlier.

"They're changing course, sir."

McNeil's excited comment brought him back to the present.

It was true. He felt a surge of relief, almost of triumph, as he saw the two frigates, now less than a mile away, heeling over, away from the wind.

But the game was not over yet.

"Let's hope they are satisfied," he said. "If they get a view of *El Cid* beam-on they could still realise that they are being tricked."

"Not on this tack, sir," McNeil pointed out. "They'll not see her beam-on until they are past."

"And we shall have the weather station. You're right, by God. McNeil, I believe it's going to work!"

He wished he hadn't added the last comment, for it was

always bad for a captain to be proved wrong. On the other hand, there was only McNeil on the quarterdeck beside the quartermaster at the wheel and a boatswain's mate who was standing in as temporary midshipman, and McNeil was too loyal to rejoice at his captain's misjudgment.

If misjudgment it was. The French frigates were still keeping the same course, near enough for a closer inspection but far enough to make a quick run for it if the British posed a threat.

"They're not sure," McNeil said. "Let's hope they remain so, for I doubt whether any Frenchman would engage with such apparent odds against him." He paused, and then, greatly daring, added, "Unless he was inspired by the English Captain."

Penhaligon smiled. "You flatter me, McNeil. We should be fair to the captains yonder whose orders were probably to seek and probe. They'd attack quickly enough if we were alone."

"Aye, and even more quickly if we were unarmed merchantmen," McNeil added.

Penhaligon nodded. "Well, to be fair, we've done our fair share of that ourselves."

Although he was far from mercenary the thought brought him comfort, for he was not rich, scarcely well off, although he had expectations from his irascible uncle. If he married Clarissa, and that was his intention, he would need money, an estate in England—Surrey was a pleasant county and far enough away from Greystone Park to combine freedom from parental interference with a proper filial duty. Not that he disliked Sir Hubert—quite the contrary—but he was a determined old gentleman and, when troubled by gout, unpredictable. But he remembered with pleasure that Jamie would make a delightful brother-in-law.

"They're turning towards us, sir."

He watched as the leading frigate, closely followed by its companion, turned to bring the wind on her other quarter.

This could mean one or two things, either their captains were still uncertain and were coming to take a closer look, or they had recognised *El Cid* and were coming to attack.

"Two points to starboard."

"Aye, aye, sir."

He knew it was a risk, or rather an increased risk, but it was one he had to take. On the new course *Avenger* would be closing rapidly, and soon, if the French captains meant business, they would be near enough to fire. Yet having started the bluff he had to carry it through. With the protection of a ship of the line astern, this was exactly the course a probing frigate would take.

"Stand by the starboard guns!"

He had no gunnery officer, scarcely a complement of gun crews, and he knew that if he had to engage, half those crews would be needed to handle the sails.

"They're still coming, sir."

He watched grimly, expecting at any moment to see puffs of smoke from their bow chasers. Under a full spread of canvas they must be making all of five knots. He noticed with relief and pleasure that Carew, despite his reservations about the whole affair, was following suit. *El Cid*, under topsails, topgallants and main course, was coming across the wind.

Soon, at any moment now!

"They're changing course, sir; they're pulling away!" McNeil's voice was high-pitched with excitement.

"So they are, by God!"

He watched as the French frigates heeled, with bow waves foaming, and then, with the wind on their quarter, continued westwards.

THIRTEEN

Avenger, escorting her much larger prize, sailed under top-sails and reefed course into Mahon Sound. It was a glorious morning, typical of early summer in these parts, with the wind, which blew unchecked by the low hills during the winter, now gentle and warm. There was a scent of flowers and wood smoke, and the almond trees which bedecked the lower hills and the gorse which spread across the scrubland beyond were in full blossom. On the quay was a crowd of well-wishers, among whom he could see Meldrum and Hard-castle and two of the midshipmen. Three of the prizes they had taken were still in port.

And there was Clarissa.

He saw her as, with topsails backed, *Avenger* glided towards the quay. She stood beside her brother in an open carriage, her hand waving ecstatically and her pert, lively face broadened by a grin. The very sight of her gladdened his heart in a way no other woman had managed. She was adorable.

As helpers on the quay, including some of his own crew who had been waiting in port for *Avenger*'s return, tied up he went through the entry port and, without waiting for the gangway, leapt ashore.

"Cocky! Cocky, darling!"

She was out of the carriage and into his arms before he had taken a few strides, and, unmindful of the crew who were watching with lively interest, kissed him on the lips.

"Clarissa!"

"Have you missed me?"

"Not a bit. I've been too busy."

"Oh!" She slapped his arm. "Well, I've missed you. I've been thinking about you all the time." She kissed him again, smothering his rejoinder.

"Not all the time," a voice said. "I've been teaching her something of seamanship."

"Jamie!" Without releasing Clarissa, he extended an arm and, grinning broadly, shook hands with her brother. "It's good to see you."

"It's good to see you, Cocky, especially to see you returning in triumph."

"What?" He turned to watch Carew bringing *El Cid* alongside. "An antiquated, badly run ship of the line. I doubt that she'll be of much use except as scrap."

"She could still have blown you out of the water."

"If she had ever fired her guns."

"She's a marvellous ship," Clarissa said, "and I shall insist that Daddy has her sold for her proper value." She looked up at him with a loving smile and wrinkled her nose as his arm tightened on her shoulder.

"Clarissa's right," Jamie said. "You've not done badly for yourself with—what is it?—five or six prizes from one voyage."

"If I can persuade that old skinflint Murdo to assess them properly."

"Don't worry," Clarissa said. "From what I heard, Mr Murdo is a changed man since you had words with him. He's too much afraid of you and mindful of Daddy to cheat."

"I hope you're right."

"Now if you can bear to tear yourself from your ship for a moment," Clarissa began, and then stopped. Her eyes, which sometimes, when she was assuming an innocent expression, seemed almost too big for her face, opened even wider. She had just seen the marquesa.

Following her gaze, Penhaligon took his arm from her shoulder. "Good God! I'd forgotten."

Without a word of explanation, he left Clarissa and her brother and hurried up the gangway. He smiled, contritely, as he took the marquesa's arm. "My apologies, ma'am—just back in port—so much to do."

"So I see."

She looked very beautiful. Despite the confined area of the cabin and its limited facilities for toilet, she had somehow contrived to bathe and dress and brush her hair so that she could have walked without comment into any social gathering in Barcelona or Madrid. With her fingers resting on his arm, she trod carefully down the gangway.

"Marquesa!" It was Jamie, thunderstruck, who cried out.

"You know each other?" Penhaligon was surprised.

"Yes—that is—"

"I told you, captain," the marquesa said, "that there were things about me that would surprise you."

"Yes, but—"

"Have you had much chance to know each other?" Clarissa asked, in a small, tight voice.

"On the contrary, my dear," the marquesa replied. "The captain has been too busy fighting to spare time for even the common courtesies. I warn you, my dear, since you clearly think well of him, that his manners are deplorable."

"So are mine," Clarissa replied, cheerfully, "so that's all right."

The marquesa nodded and smiled, not unkindly, and looked from one to the other until Jamie, who was clearly much taken aback by the encounter, remembered his manners. "Marquesa, forgive me. May I introduce my sister, Clarissa. Clarissa, the Marquesa de Cullera y Alicante."

"*Enchanté.*" The marquesa graciously inclined her head and smiled.

"You speak French as well as English?" Clarissa asked.

"A small accomplishment, my dear. I learnt French because my sister married the Duc de Mortemar. I learnt English for

want of something better to do. I'm afraid there is not much
to occupy the mind in a small village in Valencia."

"Except riding the lemon packet occasionally," Penhaligon
suggested.

She smiled and touched his arm. "That was a long time
ago."

They drove to the house on Gallows Hill, Clarissa and
the marquesa facing Penhaligon and Jamie across the carriage.
The streets were busy, for it was still early morning, and
Clarissa and Penhaligon exchanged secret, loving glances and
quick smiles when they saw housewives haggling over loaves
and oranges and squawking hens; workmen, brown of arm
and face, pushing trucks, sweeping paths, hawking, shouting,
arguing; and children, even browner than their parents,
playing in the fountain. At the street corners donkeys, laden
with peppers and melons and strings of onions, waited with
heads bent, while along the street mules, flicking ears against
the flies, plodded between the shafts of gaily painted carrettas.

As they left the town Penhaligon noticed quite by chance—
his eyes were following a pretty girl—the fat, respectable
figure of Murdo, the assessor.

When they reached the house Clarissa took the marquesa
away to her bedroom, but it was not long before she escaped
and came running down the stairs, across the hall, where she
all but knocked over the butler, and into the sitting-room
where Penhaligon was talking with Jamie.

"Cocky!" She flew into his arms and covered his face with
kisses. "Cocky! I've missed you so."

Jamie, with an indulgent smile, said, "Well, if you'll excuse
me—" and left them to it.

Penhaligon drew her down beside him on the settee and
with one arm round her shoulders traced with his finger the
contours of her face : nose, eyelids, ears, the delicate curve of
her chin. He kissed her once, then once again, and a third
time for luck. Her eyes looking into his were brown and

trusting, her smile, soft and tremulous, was never far from a grin.

"Cocky! What do you think of the marquesa?"

He shrugged. "What should I think? She's a beautiful woman."

"More beautiful than me?"

"Oh, much more." He laughed and kissed her again to stifle her protest.

"Cocky." She was suddenly small and vulnerable. "You didn't—?"

He smiled. "What a funny girl you are. I love you. Don't you understand? There'll never be anyone else."

"Not even for pleasure?"

"Not even for pleasure."

She sighed contentedly and snuggled even more deeply into his arms. "Oh, Cocky, I love you so."

Lunch was taken on the verandah, a broad, vine-covered extension to the southern side of the house, with a magnificent view of the town and harbour and the blue inlet from the sea. Sir Hubert, who was having one of his better days, was charming, even jovial, and obviously much taken with the marquesa. To Penhaligon he was warm and friendly. As a sherbet pudding followed the bouillabaisse and curried squid and veal and roast beef, which as the marquesa observed, with no more than a hint of condescension, was typical of the Englishman abroad, the talk turned to Napoleon. Sir Hubert, who, despite his customary bouts of ill-humour, was a gentleman, had until now studiously avoided any mention of the war in deference to the feelings of his guest In fact, it was the marquesa herself who broached the subject.

"You have been most kind, Sir Hubert, not to mention the war, but I wonder, since your son appears not to have told you, whether you know my feelings about Bonapart?"

"No, ma'am, but if it causes you embarrassment—"

"Not embarrassment, Sir Hubert, but rather caution."

"I don't understand."

"I *hate* Napoleon, I hated the Commune, sometimes I think I hate the French."

"Then you are one of us!" Clarissa exclaimed.

"That is more true than you think, my dear," the marquesa said. "I think—" She turned to Jamie. "May I be allowed to explain?"

The glances that passed round the table were like signals in a sea action. Well? What do you think? Is it safe? Only Clarissa was left out.

"I think, my dear," Sir Hubert said, to his daughter, "that it is only fair that we should explain. Your brother, for the last six months or so, has been playing a lonely and dangerous role. Ostensibly, as you know, he left the Navy. Ostensibly he has developed a passion for plants and funguses; this passion takes him about Europe."

Clarissa said, "Oh, I know all about that, Daddy. You mean that Jamie isn't really a plant-hunter at all: he's a spy."

"Ssh!"

Seeing her father's surprise and consternation, she was instantly contrite. "Sorry, Daddy! I'd forgotten I'm not supposed to know."

"How did you find out? Jamie?"

"Not me, Father."

"No one told me, Daddy. I worked it out for myself." She gestured with her hands and said, "It was such a feeble story —I mean about Jamie's plant-hunting. He's my brother! We grew up together. Jamie wouldn't know a daisy from a buttercup."

"Don't you be too sure, my girl!" Jamie admonished. "Since I've started this game I've learnt more than you imagine."

"Well, even so, you'd never be clever enough to be a botanist."

"I'm as clever as you, my girl, and not half as cheeky."

"All right! All right!" Sir Hubert stopped the squabble

before it developed. "In fact, you are quite right, my dear. Jamie, being not only an excellent linguist but a brave young man, volunteered to become a British agent, and that's what he has been doing since he left the Navy."

"Your health, Jamie!" Penhaligon said, raising his glass. "Your father is right, in fact he does you less than justice: you are a very brave man."

Jamie laughed and went red and looked embarrassed. "Nothing brave about it," he said, "not when one works with someone like the marquesa."

He paused and looked at the marquesa, as though asking her permission to continue, and in fact it was the marquesa herself who explained.

"I am Spanish," she said, "at least three-quarters Spanish. My grandmother was Lady Winchester and my nurse who came with her from England taught me your language. My sister married a Frenchman, the Duc de Mortemar, and was guillotined with him in the Terror."

Sir Hubert sighed and shook his head. "I am sorry, my dear, for this must be very painful to you."

"Painful, yes, Sir Hubert, but not in the way you imagine. My emotions, when I allow myself to think of them at all, are not of sorrow, but of anger." She looked across the table and her appearance seemed to change. Her soft, voluptuous body, her dark eyes and red lips were forgotten. Instead she became as hard as a *sans-culotte*. She said, "I only want one thing, Sir Hubert: I want revenge."

Sir Hubert put his glass on the table. "So you are working for us?"

"Isabelita—" Jamie began, and then stopped, as though conscious that this was the first time they had heard her name. "Isabelita has a castle in Valencia. It is built on a headland overlooking the sea."

"A perfect position for observation," the marquesa continued, "for there is nothing which passes along that coast which I, or my assistants, do not see."

"And this information is passed to Jamie?" Sir Hubert asked.

"That is so. Your son makes regular visits—but you probably know that."

"On *Heldstrom*," Sir Hubert said to Penhaligon. "The vessel you thought was spying for the French."

Penhaligon nodded but did not reply.

"I get other information," the marquesa said, "for my husband has a government appointment in Madrid. When he comes home he tells me what is happening."

"Knowing that you will pass it on to the English?" Penhaligon asked.

"Goodness, no!" She laughed. "He is a loyal Spaniard."

"But you can persuade him?"

"Captain Penhaligon," she said, "I am a woman, perhaps even a beautiful woman. My husband loves me. There is no difficulty."

Penhaligon met her eyes. "You are very determined."

"Yes."

He said, "This watch you keep. Who is doing it now?"

"At this moment?" she looked at him in surprise. "I don't know. I expect the castle is in such an uproar following my disappearance that no one is doing what he should be."

"But at other times, say last week. You can't be looking all the time."

"No. I have an assistant."

"One assistant? I thought you said 'assistants'."

She looked at him coldly, and Sir Hubert at the head of the table moved impatiently. "Is this an interrogation, captain?" she asked.

Penhaligon smiled and spread his hands. "I am sorry, if that's how it seemed. It's just—well, I am so intrigued by your story. I find it fascinating."

"It is fascinating," Jamie put in. "Isabelita is a remarkable woman."

She smiled and inclined her head. "Thank you."

"This assistant," Penhaligon continued, ignoring Sir Hubert's glare and the marquesa's raised eyebrows. "Is it someone you can trust?"

"Completely. I would not be such a fool as to put my life at risk, captain. I trust her completely."

"It's your nurse, then. Am I right?"

She nodded. "It is my nurse."

"Who must be over eighty."

"She is eighty-four."

"Really, Penhaligon," Sir Hubert exploded. "I can't see what you're getting at."

"I'm not getting at anything, Sir Hubert. My only concern is for the marquesa—and Jamie. It seems to me that they are both taking considerable risks. If the old lady, the nurse, should be suspect, if she should drop a hint, perhaps quite unwittingly, their lives would be worth nothing."

"She won't betray me," the marquesa said, smugly. "She loves me too much."

"I am glad to hear it," Penhaligon smiled at her, but no one, except perhaps Clarissa, who loved him, saw that he was only smiling with his lips. "I don't suppose that in your vigils you have seen anything of *Gironde*?"

"But of course—at least—" She looked puzzled. "I understood that she was engaged by a British vessel—with your ship *Avenger*, or so my husband told me."

"That is correct."

"And *Gironde* came off second best. The French were furious."

"She lost a yard and was holed quite badly. Last time we saw her she was limping towards Barcelona."

"Which she reached. The necessary repairs were done. I am only repeating information I received from my husband."

"I understand." Penhaligon looked out on to the hillside as he thought. The sun was high now, and heat was shimmering above the bushes, the bougainvillea and gorse and oleander, and above the red roofs of town. There was a sea mist on the horizon, and, nearer, the outline of the low hills with their orchards and scrubland and lonely pines was blurred. "You've not heard of *Gironde* since?"

"Not heard of her; I've seen her."

He stared at her with eyes that saw defeat. "Seen her? You mean she's at sea again?"

"She passed a week ago, heading south."

"For Gibraltar," Sir Hubert said. "She'll play havoc with our shipping there."

Penhaligon frowned, half rose, then sat down again. "I must go, Sir Hubert, as soon as possible. I must put to sea again."

"Oh, Cocky!" Clarissa's face was woebegone.

"Very well," Sir Hubert said, "if you must. At least let us finish lunch."

"Of course. I'm sorry."

"In any case, you can't sail until you have re-victualled. I doubt that you'll get it done tomorrow."

"I'll get it done. I shall sail tomorrow evening, or the following dawn at the latest."

Sir Hubert sighed. "What energy! What enthusiasm! When I was a young man, you wouldn't have torn me so easily from the company of pretty women."

Penhaligon looked at Clarissa and said, "The sooner I leave, sir, the sooner I shall return. I hope that Clarissa will be waiting."

"If you are not too long." She smiled to hide the trembling of her lips.

"What about me, captain?" the marquesa asked. "If you are going south, you must pass near Cullera. Could you bear my company for another day?"

Penhaligon bowed stiffly. "It would be a pleasure, ma'am. In view of the unhappy circumstances of your abduction it's the least I can do."

He was smiling, but Clarissa, who was watching closely, saw his expression change. There was a hard look in his eyes as he leant across to her and whispered, "Keep talking!"

If she was startled she did not show it, for she continued, in a cheerful voice, "I hope he gets you back safely, marquesa, and doesn't indulge in any fights on the way. I'm sure, from all I've heard, that he is unnecessarily quarrelsome and could easily avoid many of these engagements if he wished."

While she talked and the others at the table stared, Penhaligon rose quietly and walked round the table.

"But at least he brought you here safely," Clarissa went on, "so there's a reasonable chance that he will get you back, only if there's so much as a sniff of a French ship—"

Penhaligon had reached the door. He took the handle and jerked it open, and had to step quickly aside to avoid the tumbling body beyond.

FOURTEEN

"THOMAS! What the devil does this mean?"

Sir Hubert was on his feet, and the anger in his voice and in the almost purple texture of his face were at least partly due to the physical discomfort of rising. The rich meal, the wine, the long period of sitting, talking, remembering his manners, had all stoked the fires of his irascibility. He was overdue for an explosion.

"Sir!" The butler picked himself up from the floor and, with a more than reproachful look at Penhaligon, straightened his jacket. "I thought you called."

"Called, damme! I didn't call: no one called! You've been eavesdropping."

"Sir?" The butler did not seem to understand. He was a man of rather less than middle age, although a certain corpulence round his waist and in the folds of his chin and a swarthiness common to men of the island made him look older.

"Listening at the door," Penhaligon explained. "Overhearing our conversation."

"No, sir!" The man put on an offended expression, although the pallor of his cheeks and the uncertainty of his bearing, as though with only a small amount of pressure he might bolt, belied his indignation.

"Then what were you doing there, damme?" Sir Hubert insisted.

"I told you, sir. I thought you called."

Sir Hubert screwed up his face as though, despite the ladies present and his own dignity as flag officer commanding, he could not contain himself much longer, but then, not trusting himself to speak, nodded to Penhaligon.

"How long have you been there?" Penhaligon asked.

"Sir?"

"How long were you at the door?"

"A minute, sir—I had just come. I heard nothing."

"Except someone call."

"Yes, sir."

"So, where were you standing?"

"In the hall, sir."

"You were standing in the hall and you heard, or thought you heard, someone calling—through the closed door, across the drawing-room? You must have remarkable hearing."

"Yes, sir. Thank you, sir."

"And was your hearing good enough to hear us talking about the war?"

"No, sir. I heard nothing."

Penhaligon seemed suddenly to lose interest. "Very well." He said casually to Sir Hubert, "The man's probably telling the truth, sir. It's of no consequence."

"What?" Confused and even disappointed that he was to have no further chance to vent his spleen, Sir Hubert sat down.

"Very well, Thomas—only next time wait until I call— and when you reach the door, knock. Is that understood?"

"Yes, sir."

As the man withdrew, Penhaligon came round the table again and sat down. He knew that they were all looking at him, Sir Hubert and Jamie confused, Clarissa trusting; only the marquesa seemed to be watching with calculating eyes.

"I must say, Cocky, you're easily satisfied," Jamie said. "The fellow was plainly listening."

"Perhaps. In any case, what could you do?"

"Do?" Sir Hubert said. "I'd have him whipped, that's what I'd do. If I thought he was spying, I'd have him shot."

"Without proof, sir? He could have been telling the truth —it's possible."

Sir Hubert moved impatiently in his chair. "Well, if that's what you think. But I tell you one thing; I'll watch what I say before him in future."

"I think that would be wise, sir."

"Well," Clarissa said, folding her hands before her on the table and giving her elfin smile, "that's that. I thought we were in for some excitement."

"What clothes does he wear?" Penhaligon asked.

"Who? Thomas? Well, you just saw."

"I mean when he goes out."

"I don't know. I suppose what every servant wears." Clarissa was still confused.

"He wears a cloak," Jamie said, "a cloak and a billycock hat."

With the meal scarcely over and Sir Hubert, assisted by Clarissa, hobbling off for his afternoon nap, Penhaligon was already eager to return to *Avenger*. Jamie, who had not seen his friend for a long time and was anxious to hear his news, asked if he could accompany him, and after making their apologies to the marquesa, who seemed quite happy to remain on the verandah, they set off.

"Shall we take the carriage?"

"For God's sake, Jamie, it's only half a mile and all downhill. Let's walk."

They had scarcely crossed the lawn before they heard a cry, "Cocky!", and turned to see Clarissa running after them.

"You're not going? You're not going to leave me?" Her face puckered, her lips drooped at the corners like the expression of a disappointed child.

"I must." Penhaligon put his hand on her shoulder and kissed her gently. "I'll be back this evening—if I may."

"As soon as you can."

"Why not stay with us while you're here?" Jamie asked.

"It will be no trouble. Your steward can bring up your dunnage."

"It will only be for two nights—one if I can prod some life into those loafers at the victualling yard."

"Cocky!" Clarissa took his arm and looked up at him appealingly. "Make it two."

He hesitated and then, unable to resist her, smiled, "All right. I'll sail the day after tomorrow."

The dock and the victualling yard at Mahon were no more inefficient or unhelpful than the yards at any other naval ports, but Penhaligon, like any captain who begrudged his time ashore, was impatient. The dockyard superintendent, a former purser, who had perhaps been promoted beyond his ability, seemed particularly obstructive, or perhaps, as Jamie suggested, just did not understand. He was certainly slow of comprehension.

"Thirty rounds for the nine-pounders, twice that number for the eighteen-pounders. Oh, and we'll need twenty-four pounders—say, fifty—and some canister for the carronades."

The superintendent frowned and shook his head. "That's a lot of shot, sir, and I'm short-handed."

"Then I'll send some of my men."

"Yes, sir, only I don't know that I can spare—"

"Mr Smith!" Penhaligon said, forcefully. "My ship is going to sea. She is sailing at dawn, the day after tomorrow, and she will be fully equipped. I want that amount of shot and enough powder to fill the magazine on board and safely stowed away by this time tomorrow. Is that understood?"

"Yes, sir, only—" The superintendent saw the captain's expression and retreated. "I'll do my best."

On board *Avenger* the crew were making ready. The sailmaker sat with a length of canvas, one of the headsails, across his knee, the boatswain was aloft inspecting the rigging: forward, the watch on deck were painting the fo'c'sle head while others, suspended on slings, were caulking the hull. Supervising it all was McNeil, in his element where hard work, method and attention to detail were all-important, and he smiled cheerfully and saluted as Penhaligon and Jamie came aboard.

"All going well, sir. We'll be ready in good time."

"I hope so, if we can get those damned dockyard workers to move."

McNeil nodded sympathetically. He had an even lower opinion than his captain of efficiency in the yards. "When are they coming, sir?"

"Not until tomorrow, I would guess, judging from the tale of woe I heard. That reminds me, I promised to send a party to help."

"I'll have them there at dawn, sir."

"Good!" Penhaligon turned to Jamie, who was looking round with interest and a certain amount of envy, as the crew bustled to get the frigate in shape. "Fortunately, we aren't low on powder or shot. We had a fairly quiet voyage, a few shots across the bows, only one show of opposition."

"Yet you captured five prizes—six including *El Cid*—and sent another aground. You're certainly making your presence felt."

Penhaligon looked closely at his friend. "You're envious, I do declare, and I don't blame you. It's too easy. The Spaniards haven't got their hearts in this war."

"Can you blame them? They're only fighting to please Boney."

"I suppose so." He turned to McNeil and said, "We'll leave you to it, then. I'll be here in the morning when the powder comes aboard. In the meantime you had better get Hurliman to decide how he's going to stow the shot. There's probably room for most of it in the garlands."

"Aye, aye, sir."

"And this afternoon, as soon as the men have had their dinner, you'd better send another party to the victualling yard. I've had some words with the superintendent. I think you'll find he will co-operate."

Discipline or not, McNeil could not suppress a grin, which was shared by Jamie. "Aye, aye, sir."

"All the hogsheads we have below are to go back. He's agreed to change them." He pointed to the line of empty barrels which the cooper and his mates were scouring. "Water, too. We'll take as much as we can stow."

It might not be necessary to carry so much, for if they found *Gironde* it might be a short voyage—they would either capture or sink the French ship or they would be captured or sunk themselves—and there was always the chance of sending the longboat ashore, but he was determined to leave nothing to chance. *Gironde* must be destroyed.

"You have a fine ship," Jamie said, as they walked aft to the relative quietness by the taffrail.

"Yes, I've been lucky. I have some good officers, and the crew, once they accepted that I meant business, have been splendid."

"How do you get on with Carew? We know him rather well."

"He's a good officer."

"And McNeil?"

"First class."

They stood side by side with their backs to the rail, looking forward to the activity on deck and in the rigging and on the quayside, and beyond, to the hills bathed in sunshine and bright with flowers. Somewhere in the tangle of bushes goat-bells were tinkling, and gulls, wheeling overhead, uttered mournful cries.

"I was wondering," Jamie said, "if I shouldn't sail with you."

"No." Penhaligon shook his head decisively.

"Why not? It's either *Avenger* or *Heldstrom*, whenever she returns. I'd be more comfortable in *Avenger* and I'd have your company."

"Don't go back to Spain, Jamie, not for a while."

"But I must. There will be information waiting for me at

143

Cullera. Even with Isabelita away it will still be collected. It is important."

"Is it?" Penhaligon turned to face him. "Did she tell you that she had seen *Gironde*?"

"Well, no, not before this morning, but she hasn't seen me. I left on *Heldstrom*'s last return trip, five, six days back."

"She says she saw *Gironde* a week ago."

"She was mistaken: anyway, it will be in her next report."

"I'm sure it will."

Jamie looked at his friend in surprise and, because he knew him so well, with only a mild show of exasperation. "Cocky, what are you getting at? Isabelita has been good to me. She's been working for our cause, and at considerable risk. She's a brave woman."

"I'd agree with that." Penhaligon put his hand on his friend's shoulder. "There's a spy in Mahon, Jamie. Our ship movements are getting to the French and Spanish almost before we know them ourselves."

"I know that."

"Your father asked me to find him. That's what I was trying to do when I was in Mahon last time."

"So? What has this to do with Isabelita?"

"I don't know; possibly nothing."

"What about Thomas, the butler, although I admit the idea seems absurd?"

"It could be anyone, or almost anyone; Thomas, your father's secretary, Murdo the assessor, even one of the dockyard workers."

"Even me?"

"Don't joke about it, Jamie. This is serious."

"All right, only it is rather ludicrous. How could a dockyard worker get information about ship sailings?"

"How could anyone? I agree. Nevertheless, someone does."

Jamie looked at his friend and, seeing that he was serious, nodded. "All right. What is it you want me to do?"

"Stay here, or at least don't return to Spain, not until I've made a few enquiries."

"How long will that take?"

"Not long. When I return from this coming voyage I shall know."

FIFTEEN

Heldstrom returned to port next morning, and the same evening *Avenger* was ready for sea. The dock and victualling superintendents had excelled themselves, and even the workmen, spurred on by Penhaligon's vituperative tongue, had responded. As dusk was falling, Penhaligon walked with Jamie up the hill. It was a warm evening, although the clouds were low and there was a hint of rain in the air. So much the better. It was too hot for comfort, and so long as it did not take away the wind a downpour would be welcome.

"Cocky!" She met them at the gate and, mindless of her brother, threw her arms round Penhaligon's neck and held him as though she would never let him go.

"Madam!" Penhaligon said, with mock severity. "Behave yourself! We are not even affianced."

"I am," she retorted, cheerfully. "I know who I'm going to marry."

She walked between them, linking arms, and with a joyful exuberance that was irresistible, chattered and teased and squeezed the arm on her left—Penhaligon's—all the way to the house.

Dinner that evening was a happy affair, although Clarissa's mouth drooped whenever she remembered or was reminded by their conversation, especially the marquesa's, that *Avenger* was sailing at dawn.

After dinner, while Sir Hubert took his port and his gouty leg to the library, Penhaligon, partnered by Clarissa, and Jamie, partnered by the marquesa, played whist, a game which Penhaligon found difficult to understand, much less

146

enjoy. It hardly mattered. Although they lost every rubber, Clarissa was so irrepressible, teasing one moment, full of commiseration the next, that the evening passed all too quickly, and it was with regret that they heard Jamie announce that it was midnight and, since Penhaligon and the marquesa had to be on deck at dawn, it was time for bed.

Even then Clarissa would not be parted. After she had kissed Jamie and her father and had seen the marquesa to her bedroom, she ran along the passage and knocked at Penhaligon's door.

"Cocky!" Her hoarse whisper sounded clearly in his room.

"Clarissa! You'll have me in trouble." He came out into the passage and with real emotion folded her into his arms.

She was soft and yielding : her big eyes, her small oval face with the delicately pointed chin, her mouth with the urchin smile which could so quickly change to passion, her nose and her ears and her auburn hair were for him the ultimate beauty. She was perfection.

"Oh, Cocky! Cocky, darling!" As she broke from a kiss she looked up at him with eyes that were wet with tears. "Why do you have to go? Why must we be parted?"

"Don't fret." He gently stroked her hair. "I'll be back—after I have sunk *Gironde*."

"Or she sinks you. Cocky, I'm afraid."

"There's no need to be. I'll get her, she'll not escape this time."

She rested her head on his chest and for a time they remained so, without moving or speaking, each feeling the other's warmth and gentle breathing. Then she stirred.

"Cocky."

"Yes?"

"You won't forget me—tomorrow : you won't forget me?"

"What do you mean?"

"With the marquesa aboard, in your cabin—our cabin—you won't forget?" She shook her head. "She's a beautiful woman."

He put his hands on her shoulders and held her from him. "So that's what is worrying you."

She looked up at him uncertainly. "She is beautiful."

"Clarissa, look at me." He lifted her chin with his finger and looked into her eyes. "There's only one woman for me— can't you understand?" He shook his head in gentle admonition. "I love you, Clarissa. There is no one else."

When she had gone, he went to the open window and looked down over the hillside and the sleeping town. In the early moonlight he could see the line of hills, with woods, olive groves and, on the skyline, a row of pines, like dark sentinels against the sky. There were still a few lights in town, the glow of a bakery oven and, where the road met the quay, a watchman's brazier. Topmasts and rigging of *Avenger* rose above the rooftops, like pointing fingers. He looked at his watch. It was one o'clock.

When he opened his door he stood for a time in the total darkness, listening to a clock in the hall, a faint sound of snoring from one of the bedrooms and the beating of his own heart. He knew what he had to do. If he was discovered— and this was likely, even probable—there could be no explanation. He would lose everything. Yet he had to do it.

The marquesa's room was at the other end of the passage, next to Clarissa's, which made his adventure even more desperate. The only comfort he could find as he stepped carefully in the darkness was Nelson's dictum, which he would never forget : always attack.

He reached the end of the passage, waited a moment to calm his beating heart, then tapped on the door.

There was no answer, no sound of stirring within. Perhaps the marquesa was asleep.

He tapped again and almost immediately the door was opened.

"Captain!" She spoke in a whisper, realising, no doubt, that he could compromise her as well as himself.

"I must speak with you."

"What, now?"

"Please."

She hesitated a moment and then, after looking out into the passage, stood aside to let him enter.

She was in a borrowed nightgown of some transparent material, which was so much too small that it barely reached her knees. As she stood there in the candlelight watching him enquiringly but with no hint of displeasure, he was conscious of her thrusting breasts and her voluptuous body caught in the almost skin-tight embrace of the material. She could not have appeared more seductive, he thought, if she had appeared naked.

"Well?" She spoke quietly and, since he did not reply, sat down on the bed. "I presume you've not come to seduce me?"

"No." He sat beside her and laid a hand on her knee. "Not really."

"Well?" She laughed without any sign of annoyance. "Have you or haven't you? You must know."

"You are very beautiful."

"So?" She shook her head so that the dark hair swirled across her face. "You English! You may be good seamen and brave fighters, but you are such poor lovers." She took his hand and pressed it against her breast. "Now tell me what you want."

The straps of her nightgown were so tight that he tore one as he pulled it from her shoulders. She lay there, with a smile on her lips, as he pulled the taut silk from her breasts, over her thighs and then clear of her legs, but made no attempt to help. Only when she was naked did she rise and, kneeling before him, begin with expert, seductive hands to undress him.

She was a greedy and demanding lover, and an hour had passed before he could decently leave. She lay there, naked still and inviting, watching him as he dressed, and as he cast sidelong glances as her, feeling more embarrassed than he cared to admit, she was still smiling.

"I must go." He reached forward and touched her shoulder.

"Until dawn."

"An hour before dawn." He looked at his watch. "You have two hours."

"And you?" She sat up and took his arm. "Don't you ever sleep?"

"I'm a sailor. We get used to it."

"And tomorrow we'll be together, on your ship."

He said, "We must be discreet, more discreet than we've been tonight. There are no hiding places on a frigate."

"We shall find a way."

"Well," he said, again. "I must go." She still hadn't spoken. Without even bothering to throw a garment over her shoulders, she accompanied him to the door, and it was only as she held him in a farewell embrace that she asked, "What course shall we take tomorrow—south of Mallorca?"

At last!

He replied, casually, as though it was a matter of no importance, "That would be quickest, but I have to return you to Cullera—remember?"

"Of course." She kissed him again. "So, we sail north of Mallorca?"

"I expect so, depending on the wind. We'll clear Cap Formentor and set course for Cullera. You should be home in twenty-four hours, Tuesday midday at the latest."

"And then?"

"Can you ask? We shall head south under full sail and make for Gibraltar."

When he returned to his room the house was still quiet, the clock was ticking in the hall, the heavy sleeper was still disturbing the night.

He went into his room and for a time stood in the darkness with the door slightly ajar, listening.

It came sooner than he expected, the click of a door opening, a shadow moving along the passage, quiet footsteps on the stairs.

Minutes later he saw from his open window another shadow, strangely familiar in the darkness, crossing the lawn.

SIXTEEN

It was still scarcely dawn as they arrived on the quay. The low hills that flanked the Sound were still in darkness although pinpricks of light appeared from cottages and from the fires of goatherds tending their flocks, but ahead, where the hills parted to meet the sea, the sky was grey. A few civilian workmen dozed by the bollards, watched by the superintendent, who had felt constrained to see the frigate and her fiery captain out of harbour. *Heldstrom* had left her berth.

Penhaligon commented on this as, with Jamie and Smith, the superintendent, he escorted the marquesa aboard.

"Aye, they expect us to work miracles," the superintendent said, obviously talking about captains in general and perhaps, although he did not say as much, the captains of *Heldstrom* and *Avenger* in particular. "Less than a day she gave us; twenty hours to clear her, re-victual and make the turn around."

"Has she done this before?" Penhaligon asked.

"Aye, she has. Heldstrom, her captain, is unprelictable." (He had obviously heard, or mis-heard, the word somewhere and, at this hour of the morning, could think of none better.) "Four, five days she's in port usually, sometimes a week; then, when it's least convenient, he makes up his mind and—pht!— she has to be off."

As the pipes shrilled to welcome aboard, Penhaligon felt a glow of pleasure as though this, a ship of his own, with a crew moulded by discipline, example and, he hoped, loyalty, to the kind of efficiency necessary to get the best from her long, sleek lines, her impressive spread of canvas and her

151

formidable armament, was the ultimate fulfilment. He could ask for nothing better.

And yet, even as he stepped through the entry port, saluted, and nodded to McNeil, he knew that something was missing.

"Baghot," he said, "take the marquesa's dunnage below."

The marquesa, who, through the generosity of Clarissa, was leaving with two cases where she had arrived with none, held out her hand to Jamie and said, "Thank you for your hospitality—your father, too, and Clarissa: would you thank them for me?"

"Of course. I'm sorry they are not here. My father, as you know, is an old man and is frequently indisposed. Morning is not his best time."

"I understand. And Clarissa is such a child. She's probably sleeping."

Jamie hesitated and, it seemed, cast a furtive look towards Penhaligon. "I expect so."

It was the one flaw in the joy of going to sea. As Penhaligon stood on the quarterdeck where Lubbock and Rennie and young Lacey, who was midshipman of the watch, were already waiting he thought that if only she had been there, her lively face broken by a grin as she waved to him from the quayside, his happiness would have been complete. He half expected, even at this late hour, to see her emerge from the street and come running across the square, her skirt held with one hand, her face eager and her hair flying in the wind. But there was no one.

"Permission to cast off, sir?" McNeil was anxious to carry out his orders, for it was now fully dawn, the workmen on the quay were waiting, topmen by the shrouds and the watch at braces were ready. It only needed the word.

"Goodbye, Jamie," Penhaligon said. "I expect we'll be back soon. It will depend how soon we find *Gironde*."

Jamie nodded and grasped his hand. "Good luck!"

As he went down the gangway Penhaligon called after him,

"Say goodbye to Clarissa for me," but Jamie merely responded with a nod.

The crew cast off, top and headsails were hauled up and sheeted home, and, gliding like a swan over the still water, *Avenger* put to sea.

Penhaligon, a lonely figure, stood by the weather rail, watching the hills unfold, the orchards and farmsteads, the olive groves and heather-covered moorland to larboard already basking in the early warmth, the headland to starboard still in shadow. The sea was calm, although he could tell from the combers ahead that when they left the protection of land there would be a fair wind.

"Steady as she goes!"

Avenger was already making three knots, and when they cleared the headland and put on more canvas she would make eight or even nine. They should reach Cullera by dawn tomorrow.

The marquesa was standing by the larboard bulwark in the waist, her dark hair flowing and her face turned to the wind. She would have to move from there when they reached the sea, Penhaligon thought, for she had chosen the wettest part of deck. The first real waves they met would throw up enough spray to drench her, and he wondered how long she would have to spend below, changing her dress and drying and brushing her hair. Women on ships were a mistake. He shrugged. Let her find out for herself!

"We'll set a course for Formentor when we clear the cape," Penhaligon said to the master.

"Aye, aye, sir." Lubbock sniffed appreciatively, like a hound on the scent. "We'll have the wind a-beam, sir. Should make good time."

"I hope so."

Avenger was already responding to the chase, her bows dipping, bowsprit and jib boom thrusting, and her deck tilting as she reared before the waves. Crash. The hull quivered at the impact, but *Avenger* pressed on, throwing up a cloud of spray and emerging wet, decks glistening, undaunted. Thrust, plunge, rise: the relentless fight between sea and ship continued.

"Hands to make sail! All hands!"

With courses on her she plunged even deeper, emerged more doggedly and thrust her jutting prow at the horizon. It would soon be time to run out stunsails.

"Beg pardon, sir." It was Baghot disturbing his thoughts. "Young lady would like a word with you."

"What now? Where is she?"

"In the cabin, sir." Baghot lowered his eyes and grinned. " 'Fraid she got wet, sir, had to strip off. She's in what the Frogs would call *déshabillé*."

"Tell her I'll see her later. I can't come below now."

"Aye, aye, sir."

"And, Baghot, perhaps she would like some of your coffee."

They were almost clear of land now, the coastline receding with every minute, although he knew that it would remain there for the next hour or so as a dark line to starboard, and that after a relatively short period of clear horizons, Mallorca would appear to larboard. When they cleared Cap Formentor they would have the wind on their quarter.

"Is it true, sir, that *Gironde* has given us the slip, that she's south, near Gibraltar?"

Penhaligon turned and stared bleakly at Carew, who had asked the question. "I wish I knew."

"She'll do a lot of harm down there, sir, before we reach her."

"Unless another King's ship is lucky enough to reach her first."

Carew smiled. "I'm not sure, sir, with respect, that all captains would call it luck. *Gironde* could be a formidable opponent."

"Aye, but not invincible, even for a frigate. We've met her once and I've no qualms about meeting her again."

"Yes, sir," Carew replied. "It was a pity we were dismasted," and walked across to the binnacle before the captain could reply.

Towards noon they saw sail on the horizon, but it was something small, a merchantman or even a fishing boat, and Penhaligon was too impatient to investigate. The chase must continue.

They made good time throughout the day, but towards dusk the wind dropped and, even maintaining a full spread of canvas, they were all but becalmed.

"Devil take it!" Penhaligon stood holding the taffrail as he felt *Avenger* lose her rhythm; the steady pitch and upward swing were gone, and instead, as the sails, slack one moment, half-filled with some wayward gust the next, struggled to keep her moving, the helmsman, watching with anxious eyes, manoeuvred to hold a course.

Pitch and roll, pitch and roll. All around he heard the protesting creak of timber and, above, the intermittent harp of wind in the rigging. The sails flapped and bellied and went inert like a wounded soldier struggling to continue the fight.

"Beg pardon, sir, she's not holding." It was the helmsman, reporting that there was scarcely steerage way.

"Very well. Do the best you can." He considered wetting the sails, a frustrating and only partially effective exercise at the best of times, but it was nearly dark and he did not think that the wind was strong or steady enough to justify the labour. By the time whips were run through the blocks on the yards and sufficient seawater hoisted, night would have fallen in earnest and it would be difficult to continue the exercise with any degree of success. In fact, there was nothing to do but wait.

"I'm going below, Mr Carew. Call me if there's any sign of a wind."

"Aye, aye, sir."

He felt sorry for Carew, especially as, once again, he had had to deprive him of his cabin. He was a good, if rather unimaginative sailor, and under another captain, a gentleman like Lord Keith, for example, he would probably flourish. He was glad that he had been able to write a favourable report on his handling of *El Cid*.

"Captain!"

Caught by his thoughts, he had gone to his own cabin without thinking, and before he could retreat the door had opened to reveal the marquesa dressed, if that were not too strong a word, in some flimsy garment.

"I thought you would never come."

"I'm sorry. I forgot." He retreated a few steps. "I have to be on deck."

"Nonsense! There's no wind; it's dark. Don't take me for a fool, captain."

"That may be so, but—"

"Come!" She took a step into the passage, much to the delight of the sentry who was there, in the shadows, and, before he could protest, had grabbed his arm and pulled him into the cabin.

"There!" She eyed him, chidingly, thrusting out her bosom so that in the confined space between cot and bulkhead he could scarcely move without touching her. "You have been avoiding me. Why?"

He shook his head. "You don't understand. On a fighting ship a captain is on duty all the time. He must be ready."

"For what? I repeat: it is dark and there is no wind."

"The wind may return."

"So, you will feel it. Here, on the bed, you will miss nothing, the movement of the ship, the orders from above." She pointed to the deck above. "You even have a compass."

"I know." He thought desperately for some excuse she would accept. "But I must be on deck now—for the change of watch."

"At three bells?" She watched him closely and her manner changed. "I am beginning to wonder, captain, what has happened. Last night it was different, you even came to my room. You couldn't make love fast enough. Now, when we are alone, you are reluctant."

"Forgive me, ma'am, but I am a sailor. I have a duty to my ship."

"And last night?"

"We were ashore. It was a time, if I may put it so bluntly, for relaxation."

"So, you came to my room."

He smiled. "Was that so strange? You are very beautiful."

"And you were a more than satisfactory lover. Why have you changed?"

"I haven't changed, ma'am."

"Isabelita."

"I haven't changed, Isabelita: you are still very beautiful."

"Then there is no argument." She pulled the straps from her shoulders and, as the garment slipped to the floor, pressed forward against him.

It really was the change of watch when he came on deck, and he knew from the smug expression on Carew's face that his encounter with the marquesa had not gone unnoticed. There was still no wind, the sails hung limp on the yards, and the helmsman spun his wheel in vain.

"I trust you are rested, sir," Carew said, and it was impossible to see in the darkness whether he was laughing.

Penhaligon took up the slate and traverse board and examined them in the binnacle light, although they bore no information of which he was not already aware.

"Good evening, sir." It was McNeil, taking over the watch. "Are you still on deck?"

Aware that Carew was listening, Penhaligon ignored the question and pointed instead to the binnacle. "We're becalmed, Mr McNeil, as you see. God knows when we'll reach Cullera if this continues."

"It will change at dawn, sir: I'd be willing to wager. With anything like a wind we shall still be off Cullera tomorrow."

"After dark." Penhaligon nodded. "That would be an

advantage." He didn't explain and, within a few minutes of Carew's departure, went below.

McNeil, as usual when it came to weather predictions, was right. At dawn there was a sea mist, with visibility limited to a few hundred yards, but as the sun rose and the watch sweated on deck a breath of wind sprang up, enough to freshen the air, and before long there was a steady blow. Looking up at the straining yards and billowing canvas, Penhaligon felt his spirits rise. The mist was already gone, and he looked out on an empty horizon.

"Our luck's changed, sir," McNeil said. "We'll be in Cullera by nightfall."

In fact, they rounded the point and entered the northern reaches of the bay as the sun was setting, and there was still enough light to see that athough the inner harbour was crammed with small craft, the roadstead was empty. The castle, golden in the setting sun, the palm trees and the massed bougainvillea looked strangely beautiful, and even a quarter of a mile from shore they could hear the waves breaking.

"Take her in as far as she'll go with safety," Penhaligon ordered. "Have a man in the chains."

Under top and headsails *Avenger* glided shorewards, McNeil and the master and Rennie at the wheel looking anxiously ahead and listening for the leadsman's call.

"By the mark ten!" There was plenty of water still.

"By the deep nine!"

They waited impatiently as the leadsman hauled in his line, carefully looping it over his arm, and then, after a few swings, tossed it into the sea ahead.

There was a wait until the line became vertical. Then, "And a half seven." They were shoaling fast.

"That's enough," Penhaligon said, and McNeil's voice, sharp with relief, shouted, "Tops'l sheets! Tops'l clew lines!"

"Two points to larboard, Mr McNeil, if you please," and then, as *Avenger* came helm a-lee, "Back the main tops'l."

As *Avenger* hove-to less than a quarter of a mile from shore the marquesa came on deck and, shading her eyes against the sun, looked at the beach and the trees enclosing the summer house from which she had been abducted so recently. She turned to Penhaligon, who was standing beside her at the entry port, and smiled. "You have made good time, captain. I am almost sorry that our short voyage is ended."

"I share your sentiments, ma'am. It has been a pleasure." There was no point in giving her cause for suspicion at this late stage.

"Shall I see you again?"

"When the war is over—who knows? I imagine the British will always require a presence in these waters."

"Perhaps I could write to you—through Jamie."

"I would appreciate that."

The last he saw of her was sitting, straight-backed, in his gig, her dress, the rings on her fingers, her aristocratic profile and the glossy sheen of her hair clearly visible still, despite the thickening gloom.

SEVENTEEN

UNDER topsails and fore-course *Avenger* ploughed through the night. Sailing east-south-east with the wind on her beam she made good progress, and it was not long before Lubbock, the master, began to fidget. Carew, too, who had the watch, was curious, for, like Lubbock, he had been expecting a change of course this last hour. But the captain still stood alone, by the weather rail, feet astride, thinking. Was it possible, Carew wondered, unkindly, that, worn out by his amatory excursions, he had fallen asleep?

"Beg pardon, sir," he said at last, unable to contain his curiosity any longer, "but we are still on course east-south-east."

"I am aware of that."

"But, sir," Lubbock joined in, "we're forty, nearly fifty miles from land. We could clear Cap de la Nao by a margin."

"We are not going by Cap de la Nao."

"Sir?" Poor Lubbock was confused. "But if we are to head south for Gibraltar, sir, we shall have to pass the cape—sooner or later."

"We are not going for Gibraltar, in fact—" he looked at the slate, "I'll trouble you to change now, Mr Carew. Set course nor'-east by nor'."

"Nor'-east by nor', sir?"

"And get the courses on her. We'll be clawing to windward, I expect, most of the night."

It wasn't long before McNeil, who was due to take the first watch, came on deck. He had been lying in his cabin, expecting, like Carew and Lubbock, a change of course south-

160

wards, and the sudden alteration of ship's movement as she turned into the wind caught him by surprise.

"Good evening, sir." He tried to sound unconcerned, for he would never have dreamed of questioning his captain, and, since Penhaligon did not seem disposed to offer any explanation, he had to smother his curiosity with silence.

"A stiff wind," Penhaligon said; "we shall have to keep as close to it as we can."

"Yes, sir."

"Steer small!" Penhaligon called to the helmsman. "You can come round another point."

Still McNeil said nothing, although he could see that Carew, who was just about to hand over the watch, was equally curious.

Avenger battled on, thrashing through the sea, while watch on deck, already soaked with spray, huddled under the fo'c'sle head and by the main hatch, waiting the next call to wear ship. First one tack, then the other: despite the wind and the pitching decks and the sheer physical energy of hauling on sheets and braces, real progress was slow. With the wind howling through the shrouds, as though outraged that this puny ship should go against it and the cascading spray reaching as far as the quarterdeck, Penhaligon kept his lonely vigil.

"Coffee, sir?" It was not often that he was glad to hear Baghot's offer, but now, thoroughly chilled, he took the steaming mug and had drunk a mouthful of the scalding liquid before he had a chance to taste it.

He felt better for it and decided that it was unfair to keep McNeil in the dark any longer. He beckoned him to the rail, out of hearing of the helmsman and the midshipman of the watch.

"I expect you are wondering why we are on this course."

"Yes, sir, if your intention is to make Gibraltar."

"It is not." He said, "I don't believe *Gironde* is near Gibraltar, Mr McNeil. I believe she is in these northern waters, perhaps still at Barcelona."

"But our intelligence—"

"Was a trick, or so I believe, a trick to send us south."

"Leaving *Gironde* a clear field?"

Penhaligon nodded. "That's why I think, although I can't prove it except by what the lawyers call circumstantial evidence, that if we want to find *Gironde* we must sail north."

"I don't think I understand, sir."

"Look at it this way: where do you think *Gironde* could hurt us most—in the long run?"

"In the south, or so I would have thought. With all our ships coming through the Straits, she could make a fine haul."

"Yes, but for how long? Don't forget our strength in those waters. We have Cadiz and Malta under siege. Every British ship of war puts in at Gibraltar. Admiral Nelson's fleet is at Naples but could easily sail westwards. Lord Keith will surely return soon from Brest. *Gironde* would cause damage all right, but for how long? Her end would be certain."

McNeil considered the point and then broke off just long enough to shout fresh orders.

"Wear ship! Hands to wear ship!"

When he came back to the taffrail he had his answer. "I see what you mean, sir, and, of course, you could be right. With *Avenger* out of the way *Gironde* would have easy pickings."

"Exactly. And think of all the other advantages. If things went wrong, if the British sent a squadron or even another ship of the line to match her she has only to run for Toulon or Marseilles or Barcelona. She might never be caught."

"Well, she'll be caught now," McNeil said, with a smile. "She'll not escape *Avenger*."

When dawn came they were still sailing close-hauled and they were, according to Lubbock, although they could not see land, some forty miles south-east of Cap de Tortosa. This, Penhaligon thought, was on the approximate course *Gironde* would sail if, contrary to his judgment, she headed south, and within sight from masthead of any course she would be likely to take if, as he believed, Lamartin intended to hunt these northern waters.

It was a question of distances. Even in these narrow waters a ship, even a fleet, could pass twenty to twenty-five miles distant, just over the horizon, and not be seen. It had happened to Nelson before his famous victory at the Nile when the whole Toulon fleet of thirteen ships of the line, four frigates and two hundred transports had passed so close that even one scouting frigate on the British side would surely have found it and, since Bonaparte himself was aboard, could have altered the whole course of history.

He would not let such ill-luck happen to him, although the only practical steps he could take were to put his best men as look-outs at the mastheads and to guess, and guess correctly, the course Lamartin might take.

Avenger continued north-east by north into a wind which showed no sign of abating and, indeed, as the day wore on grew stronger. Refusing to shorten sail, Penhaligon was forced to watch *Avenger* crashing into seas that thrust her back and sometimes threatened to engulf her and caused her to ship so much water that the pumps were going constantly.

By dusk *Avenger* was off Tarragona and, following the line of the coast, altered course two points to starboard, bringing the wind from the bow to nearer a-beam, to the easier passage of the ship and the relief of a weary crew. During the night she passed Barcelona.

On the morning of the third day Penhaligon came on deck to yet another empty horizon, although Lubbock assured him that Palamos was no more than thirty miles to larboard, and, since they would soon be passing into French waters, he had to consider his next move.

The trouble was, he could not be sure that *Gironde* was actually at sea. The merchant captain they had taken earlier had spoken of serious damage, of *Gironde* being out of the water and facing repairs of weeks or even months. But whatever the damage, unless it was too serious for repair, she must be ready now. The question was, had she slipped out already? Was she somewhere in these waters, or had the marquesa been telling the truth when she said that she had sailed for Gibraltar?

Penhaligon was a cool and successful gambler and he, more than most captains, who learnt and accepted without question the seamanship of their elders, knew how necessary it was to back a hunch, especially when luck was running for you. Nelson, who until their recent meeting in Naples he had admired from afar, knew this and acted on it and was successful. Penhaligon had believed, and still believed, that *Gironde* was in these waters. *Avenger* must search until she found her.

The resolve was easier to make than to carry out. Entering the Gulf of Lions, which lapped the marshy, inhospitable coast of southern France, they saw more and more shipping, small merchantmen mostly, brigs and brigantines, luggers, topsail schooners and yawls. They saw fishing boats so small that he could only admire their skippers who would venture so far from land. They saw one ship of war, a frigate, which altered course so rapidly when they were sighted that she was never more than hull down on the horizon. But there was no sign of *Gironde*.

"Like a proverbial needle in a haystack," McNeil observed, as another day passed without success. As an older man and one who was clearly sympathetic, McNeil had been accepted by the captain as the one person to whom he could talk; in fact, in his lonely watches on the quarterdeck Penhaligon had come to welcome the common sense and measured words of his elderly lieutenant.

"The trouble is," Penhaligon confessed, "that unless we find her soon we shall lose our biggest advantage."

"Surprise?"

"Exactly. These merchantmen we've seen and not molested and the frigate we saw today will report back to land and somehow—they'll find a way—*Gironde* will be alerted."

"Unless they think that because they haven't been molested

we can't be *Avenger*," McNeil suggested. He smiled and said, without any hint of sycophancy, "They've a great respect, sir, for the English Captain."

Penhaligon smiled in return. "I hope you are right. And, I must confess, it hurts, physically hurts, to pass by these fat merchantmen that could make our fortunes, but I'll not be diverted. Nothing shall stop us until we find *Gironde*."

"I'm sure the men understand that, sir. They want *Gironde*, too. And they are not ungrateful for what you have done for them already. There's no one, from the bo'sun to the youngest loblolly boy, who won't take home a tidy sum."

A fourth day passed and a fifth, and since they had now sailed as far east as Toulon he decided to turn about and make a further search in the waters they had already covered.

It was seven bells in the afternoon watch when Larsen on the maintop hailed the deck.

"Ahoy, deck!"

"Yes?" Penhaligon was at the rail and calling up through cupped hands before Carew, who was officer of the watch, could move. "Maintop, what do you see?"

"Can't rightly tell, sir—something small. Could be a dinghy."

"What's her position?"

"On the starboard bow, sir."

"Larboard your helm, Mr Carew. We'll take a look."

The mysterious object which soon became visible from deck proved on closer inspection to be a spar. Fastened to it by ropes, like limpets to a ship's bottom, were two seamen.

"Heave-to, Mr Carew. Lower away my gig."

It was Lovegrove who was rowed across to investigate and who returned after a short time with two bodies—whether dead or alive, Penhaligon could not tell—and as he came alongside called up, "One's alive, sir, but only just—the other's dead and, by the looks of it, for some time."

"Bring them both up, Mr Lovegrove. No, wait! I'll lower away a sling."

The English Captain

He knew that it was sentimental poppycock to bring the body aboard—the dead were dead and had no use for sympathy—but he also knew, better than most, the feelings of the crew. Thieves, murderers, vagabonds they might be, yet they set a store on propriety and the correct order of things. A dead man, especially a dead seaman, deserved a Christian burial. Very well, their feelings should be respected.

The man who had been pronounced alive proved to be one of their own kind, a seaman from *Defiant*, a British sloop of war, attacked and sunk only two days earlier by a French ship of the line. The seaman, who despite his long immersion and seemingly poor condition revived quickly enough after a stiff measure of rum, said that he didn't know the name of their attacker—it had happened unexpectedly, soon after dawn—but thought, from what he had overheard from the quarter-deck that she had a name something like "*Jee-ron*".

EIGHTEEN

UNDER plain sail *Avenger* thrashed westwards before a quartering wind. A night and a day had passed since they had picked up the seaman, and another dusk was falling as Penhaligon scanned the horizon.

Gironde must be here! She must be in these waters. There was no possibility that she could escape.

Yet, even as he gave himself the comforting assurance he knew that it was not true. Once again *Gironde* might have passed during the hours of darkness or even in daylight if she were no more than a few sailing hours away. He remembered McNeil's simile: like a needle in a haystack.

"Permission to shorten sail, sir?"

"What?" He turned from his gloomy thoughts to Carew, who was standing before him. "No, not yet. There's still another half-hour of daylight."

"Aye, aye, sir."

Once again he felt sorry for Carew, who, despite his unfortunate manner, was a good sailor. Of course he was right to suggest a reduction in canvas; no captain in his right mind maintained a full spread at night, for apart from the possibility of collision—and no one could say that any stretch of navigable water was empty—there were the further hazards of sudden changes of weather. The East Indiaman *Calcutta* had broached to in the hours of darkness less than a year ago, caught in a sudden squall, and even if a weather change could be foreseen the danger and unpleasantness of handling canvas, sustained only by a foot-rope and a swaying yard a hundred feet or more above the deck was not to be ordered lightly. Yet he had to find *Gironde*.

From their position at noon, which he had checked with McNeil and Lubbock, they were now less than a hundred miles from the Spanish coast, and he wondered, if *Gironde* was still ahead, whether Lamartin was making for Barcelona.

There was only one way to find out.

"We'll keep a full spread of canvas, Mr Carew, unless the weather changes. She's riding well enough as she goes."

"Aye, aye, sir—and when it's dark?"

"We'll keep her as she is."

He knew that Carew thought he was mad and that he was praying for the time when he could hand over the watch to Meldrum, a solid North Countryman who accepted all orders, good or bad, without question. Following him, for the graveyard watch, would be McNeil, who also had too much regard for his captain to demonstrate.

Pitch and thrust, pitch and thrust: it was exhilarating to stand by the weather rail, feeling the regular downward and upward tilts of the deck, the dash of spray in the face and the rumbustious onslaught of the wind. The sea ahead was lost in darkness except for the occasional comber, and, such was *Avenger*'s speed, the bow wave was still creaming as it passed the stern. Rennie at the wheel seemed to have no qualms about the canvas they were carrying, for his face, caught by the binnacle light and wet with spray, showed the composure of a helmsman holding a steady course with a wind on the quarter.

"Mr Carew," Penhaligon called. "Send a reliable look-out forward with a night glass and speaking-trumpet."

It would give a measure of safety provided the look-out was sharp-eyed and quick-witted enough, but he knew that he was doing it for Carew rather than for himself: at nine knots the chances of avoiding a collision would still be small.

The night passed: Meldrum took over from Carew and McNeil from Meldrum. It was not until six bells in the graveyard watch that Penhaligon went below.

He doubted whether he would sleep, for he was too con-

scious of the wind in the rigging, the steady rise and fall of
the deck and the continual creak of timbers to forget even for
a moment that *Avenger*, sailing almost blind, was plunging
through the night. Baghot, who seemed to anticipate his movements with an almost uncanny prescience, met him in his
cabin and without waiting for an order guided him firmly to
his cot, took off his shoes and jacket, and turned down the
lamp. Within minutes Penhaligon was asleep.

He awoke while it was still dark and, annoyed at his own
weakness, rose so quickly that he almost stunned himself on
the deck beams.

"Baghot!"

He was still rubbing his head when his steward entered.

"You're awake, sir. I'll get you some coffee."

"Belay that! I must get on deck. Pass me my shoes."

"Two hours, sir, that's all you've had," Baghot said, as he
knelt by the cot. "Two bells just sounded, wind's nor'-nor'-east
and fresh, and Mr Carew has the watch."

Penhaligon nodded as he slipped on his jacket. From the
compass he saw that their course was still steady on nor'-east
by east. If the wind was still holding, they must be nearing
the coast of Spain.

"Rouse Mr Lubbock and ask him to meet me on deck."

As he climbed the companion to the quarterdeck he saw
that the sky over the larboard quarter was already tinged with
grey. The wind had abated a little, although the canvas was
still taut, and the deck movement was hardly less pronounced.
A sudden flurry of spray stung his face.

"Good morning, sir." Carew touched his hat and moved
away for the captain to inspect the slate. He looked far from
happy, although there was a note of relief in his greeting.
"Twenty minutes to dawn, sir."

Penhaligon nodded. He wanted dawn to come—desperately, and yet he felt a certain reluctance to lose the cover
of night. Another dawn, with another empty horizon, would
be almost more than he could bear.

169

"You sent for me, sir?"

"Yes, Mr Lubbock. Take the slate and traverse board and tell me our position."

"I can do that, sir, right away. I was up here only minutes ago with Mr Carew's permission. Begging your pardon, sir, but we are off the Gulf of Rosas, just over the frontier, so to speak."

"Are we in sight of land?"

"Almost, sir, but not quite. By my reckoning we're twenty-five miles, or possibly less, from Cap de Creus."

"Thank you, Mr Lubbock."

When the master had gone, Carew came across to the taffrail. "It will soon be light, sir."

"I know." He spoke calmly, almost indifferently, for he was determined not to let Carew sense his misgivings.

"We could be running close to land, and if Lubbock's calculations are wrong—"

"They're not." He relented a little and added, "I checked them myself yesterday noon."

"Yes, sir, but during the night—"

His further complaint was stifled by a call from the bows. "Captain, sir! There's something ahead."

"That's it, sir!" Carew exclaimed. "It's land or another ship."

"Quiet!" As he put the glass to his eye he was quite calm. Whether Lubbock's calculations were wrong, which he didn't believe, or by ill-luck they were on collision course with another ship, there was no excuse for panic. *Avenger* still had the wind, she had a look-out in the bows: forewarned, he could guard his ship from danger.

"Sail ho! Sail on the starboard bow!" The cry came from the masthead.

Penhaligon lifted his face to the direction of the disembodied voice. "Masthead, what do you see?"

"Green larboard light, sir."

"How far ahead?"

"Can't see, sir. There's something there, sir—just a shadow."

"Very well. Tell me when she's clearer." He turned and said, in as casual a tone as he could manage, "Mr Carew, beat to quarters, please. Clear for action."

At the boatswain's shout the drum rolled, petty officers dived into the fo'c'sle, swishing their rattans, the crew below came tumbling aloft, some dressing, some still half-asleep, although a whip of spray from the cutwater and the even sharper cut of the boatswain's cane soon brought them to wakefulness, the officers ran up to the quarterdeck, the gunner was assembling his crews.

"Mr Lovegrove! Faster with those buckets!"

The gun breechings were off, men were ready at tackles, the gunner was making his way to the magazine.

"Mr Simmons! Get some waisters to work with that sand."

Markedly composed in the general well-organised mêlée, the marines formed up by the gangway to be inspected by their officer who, in a moment, ordered them to break ranks and to disperse, moving smartly but not running, to the hatchways and the waist. Through his glass Penhaligon could see the dim shadow of a vessel ahead.

It had occurred to him in that first shock of surprise that she might be approaching on an opposite course (the single light meant nothing: the larboard side could be hidden on either tack), but if this were so she would be in sight by now and might even have passed. "A point to starboard, Mr Rennie." The green light was clearly visible now.

What was happening on the other ship, he wondered. Had she seen *Avenger*'s lights before he had given the order to cover them? Was she, too, preparing for action, knowing that when daylight came the ship astern would have the weather gage? Had the sound of *Avenger* preparing for action carried on the wind? If so, it was strange that she still carried a light.

"Permission to load, sir?"

"Carry on, Mr Meldrum. Load and run out."

The sky astern was flooding with yellow.

171

"Deck there! I can see her now, sir. She's a ship of the line—a Frog, unless I'm mistaken."

Penhaligon did not even acknowledge. He had seen the ship, too, and, without troubling to use the glass, he recognised her. They had caught *Gironde* at last.

NINETEEN

Gironde had seen them—he could imagine what Lamartin would be saying to his look-outs—and as *Avenger* bore down her crew could be seen running like ants to clear for action. Even so, the French ship had yielded a massive advantage. With less than a quarter of a mile of dark, running sea between them, she was still showing only fore-course and top-gallants. *Avenger* was faster by three, probably four, knots.

"Just look at 'em!" Hardcastle exclaimed, jumping up and down like a schoolboy. "They're all sixes and sevens, they don't know what they're doing."

"They are hauling up main-course now," McNeil observed, "aye, and topsails. They'll give her some speed."

"Nothing to compare with ours," Hardcastle retorted. It was amazing what confidence one action could give, thought Penhaligon.

"Shall I try with the bow chaser, sir?" Meldrum called.

"Very well, Mr Meldrum. It will give them something to think about."

Usually he hated to fire at long range, for with the imperfect science of gunnery in those days even a carefully laid broadside was largely a matter of hit or miss. A single shot fired from a heavy fo'c'sle head would depend far more on luck than any skill of the gunner. The only effective way of fighting, he had decided long ago, was at close range, a cable's length at most, with all the weight of metal you could muster, and with a captain alert and skilful enough to use the wind to advantage, to manoeuvre from danger and as quickly return to the attack.

"Fire!"

Almost at once the crew of the forward gun gave him the lie. The nine-pound shot soared into the air—they could actually follow its flight—landed on *Gironde*'s poop and after scoring a smouldering line across the deck crashed with spectacular effect into one of the maindeck guns.

A cheer went up from *Avenger*'s crew, a splendid boost for morale at the beginning of action, Penhaligon thought.

"Get ready your larboard guns, Mr Meldrum!"

Gironde, he saw, was edging back her topsail, encouraging *Avenger* to pass. Well, two could play at that game.

"Stand by tops'l sheets and braces!"

Gironde was firing now, but only with her stern chaser. Her gunners were not as efficient, or perhaps as lucky, as *Avenger*'s, for although *Avenger* saw the puff of smoke and heard the report, no one saw the fall of shot.

The two ships were close now: *Gironde*'s stern was only a stone's throw away.

"Take back the main tops'l! Mr Rennie, helm a-lee!"

As *Avenger* turned, with the backed topsail acting as a brake, the larboard guns poured a hail of shot into the French ship's stern. There were cries and shouts and one piercing scream which was repeated over and over again, and then, with a speed which did credit to Meldrum's training, the guns were swabbed out, reloaded and run out in time to fire another broadside as they turned across *Gironde*'s beam.

All the advantage so far had been with *Avenger*, although Penhaligon was realistic enough to know that it could not last. Caught unawares, the French crew were still running in all directions, dousing and sanding decks, and at the same time attending to fires which had already been started, bringing up ammunition, putting on headsails, dragging dead and dying men to the mainmast. Although for a time *Avenger* had been forced to expose her beam, not a single broadside had been fired, and, indeed, the only sign of aggression at the moment was one gun, a twenty-four pounder on the maindeck, which was firing again and again, as fast as it could be swabbed out and reloaded, as much to indicate defiance, it seemed, as with any hope of success, for no one observed the fall of shot.

"Prepare to change course! Ready with tops'l braces!"

As *Avenger* turned, with the wind still on her quarter, *Gironde* had shot past and was now a quarter of a mile to leeward.

"Splendid, sir!" McNeil's eyes were shining. "She can't match us. I'll wager Lamartin is furious."

"His turn will come," Penhaligon replied.

"Aye, but we still have the weather gage."

After the first exchange when all the advantage had been with *Avenger* the odds were levelling as *Gironde*, with her guns run out and all plain sail set, turned into the wind and came towards her tormentor on the larboard tack.

Always go at 'em: Penhaligon remembered Nelson's advice. Although he could be sure of scoring with one, or possibly two, broadsides as they came down-wind, he might, by taking a calculated risk, fire his broadsides and still keep the advantage. Having your cake and eating it, as Jervis, his old mentor, had said.

Unfortunately he had used the trick before against *Gironde*. Would Lamartin be ready to thwart him if he tried it again? It was a risk worth taking.

The two ships came together on converging courses: when they met *Avenger* would get in her broadsides with one retaliatory salvo from *Gironde*, but then, if both captains followed the usual tactics, the positions would be reversed. It would be *Avenger* who would have to wear ship and come up into the wind, and it would be *Gironde* who would have the weather gage.

Unless—

"Steady as she goes! Have those larboard guns ready, Mr Meldrum!"

He could see the gun captains sweating, with teeth clenched, as they thrust and heaved the handspikes under the carriages while the crew pulled on the tackles. Others were adjusting the coigns for elevation. "First division ready, sir! Second division ready!"

The two ships were less than a hundred yards apart now, on collision course. He could see the gunners by *Gironde*'s fo'c'sle carronades, the crew at fore braces and, like toy soldiers, marines with muskets in the shrouds. He did not have to guess their target.

"Please, sir!" The quartermaster was desperate.

"Helm a-lee! Hard over! Hold her so!"

For a moment he thought Lamartin was going to fall for his trick. *Gironde*'s bows, which were now towering above them, seemed to give way, but then, perhaps as Lamartin gathered courage, they turned towards and alongside *Avenger*'s, and the two hulls met with a grinding crash.

The shock was tremendous. Penhaligon and many of the crew were thrown from their feet, and as he rose he saw that the jib boom had snapped off and, held by the headsails, was trailing in the sea. Forward, the bows and fo'c'sle head were covered with wreckage.

The damage was serious. With yards locked together, it would need only a quick order by the French commander to send boarders over *Gironde*'s much higher bulwarks to fight and overwhelm by sheer weight of numbers the bewildered Englishmen.

"Prepare to repel boarders! Mr Dexter, have your men ready!"

He had to get clear of *Gironde*. Only then could he think of the mass of timber, canvas and cordage which littered *Avenger*'s bows. He could not even stop to see what damage had been done to *Gironde*.

Then, in those first minutes of confusion, he realised something else. The guns of neither ship were firing.

"Mr Meldrum!" he shouted, and saw the gunnery officer lying on the deck, apparently dead.

"Larboard gun captains!" he shouted. "Signal if you are ready."

One hand went up, then another, other crews were shaking off the effect of the impact. "Ready, sir, number one division! Number two division ready, sir!"

"Fire on my command! Cock your locks! Ready! Fire!"

The noise was deafening, the impact so great that *Avenger* seemed to shrug, like a wrestler struggling to free from a punishing hold. For a time the hulls were clear, the helmsman spun the wheel, but then, driven by the wind, which was now on her beam, *Avenger* closed.

Again the hulls came together, although this time more gently, and in the smoke and confusion Penhaligon had time to look up at *Gironde*. Surely Lamartin would order a boarding party now. He might never have another chance.

In fact there was almost as much confusion on Lamartin's ship as on his own. Not only were the gun captains having to rally their crews, but he could see what he had not realised before: because of this point-blank range, the guns on her maindeck could not be depressed sufficiently except to fire at the difficult target of masts and rigging. Meanwhile in the darkness and even greater confusion on the gun deck, which had received the full impact of *Avenger*'s broadside, no one seemed to be in command.

"Swab out! Reload!" Penhaligon's voice was hoarse with shouting and with the smoke, bitter and pungent, which still lingered on deck. "Gun captains, signal when ready! Mr Lovegrove, get a party forward to remove that wreckage!"

"Number one division ready, sir! And number two, sir!"

"Cock your locks! Ready! Fire!"

The impact this time was even greater, perhaps because the gun captains, having recovered their senses and realising that despite the overwhelming presence of the French ship all was not lost, fired in unison to send a devastating hail of shot into *Gironde*'s hull.

The noise was beyond belief, the smell of burning powder and the smoke which enveloped the deck reminded Penhaligon, who had once, on the insistence of a classically minded uncle, read Dante, of the infamous Inferno.

"Give them another dose, lads!" Penhaligon called, and then, noticing with relief that Meldrum, who in the initial impact had been flung against a stanchion, had recovered, added, "Carry on, Mr Meldrum!"

His attention was needed for other things. The maindeck guns on *Gironde* were firing now, although intermittently, but he could not risk being dismasted. He could also see a party being mustered in *Gironde*'s waist and Lamartin, almost beside himself with frustration, urging them on. He had to get *Avenger* clear.

"Once more, Mr Meldrum, when you're ready!"

The hulls were just apart, a gap, no more than jumping distance for an agile man, between them: and they were closing.

"Fire!"

This time he could actually see the devastation caused by *Avenger*'s broadside, the smashed carriages and trunnions, the gun crews heaped in bloody messes about the deck. If he could get *Avenger* clear, the weight of metal on the two ships would be nearer equal.

"Carronade gun captains!" he shouted, realising for the first time that despite the noise and confusion his quarterdeck was comparatively quiet. "What's come over you? Get those carronades firing!"

It was not their fault. Having received no order—he realised that now—and with Meldrum out of action, they could only wait.

As more noise and an even more obnoxious cloud of smoke engulfed him he almost regretted the order, but, even before he could see, he heard the screams and shouts of wounded men on *Gironde* as the deadly grape tore among them.

"We're clear, sir!" McNeil was shouting in his ear.

"Hard a-starboard, Mr Rennie!" Penhaligon shouted, and, watching desperately, forgetful of all else, saw *Avenger* pull clear.

She had done it! He felt like shouting with relief, although he knew that they had only gained a temporary respite. Soon, as the distance between the ships widened, *Gironde*'s main-deck guns would bear.

But there was no time for speculation; there was only the immediate present.

"Go forward, Mr Hardcastle, and see what's happening to that wreckage. Take more men, from the guns if necessary, but it must be cleared."

"Aye, aye, sir."

As the young lieutenant turned and ran down the companion and along the maindeck he had time to turn his attention to the sails. To clear *Gironde*, the helmsman had had to turn *Avenger* into the wind.

"We'll have to claw our way to windward, Mr McNeil. Put her on the larboard tack."

"Hands to braces! Hands to sheets!"

As the crew hauled to bring the yards round and, through the sheets, to keep the canvas taut, *Avenger* turned, slowly at first, for she was still hampered by the trailing boom, but gathering speed as the wind caught and filled the canvas.

Next—before Penhaligon could even think of what he must do—*Avenger* was engulfed by *Gironde*'s broadside.

Lamartin, his officers, and, even more, the maindeck gun crews had sweated too long to miss the opportunity of retaliation. Shot crashed into the hull, throwing *Avenger* even more into the wind, on to the maindeck where all but one of a starboard gun crew were killed, through the sails and rigging, bringing the mizzen topgallant yard down and adding even more to the wreckage on deck, and, below, perhaps under the waterline, for the broadside had arrived as *Avenger* was heeling.

There was no time to find out. Lambert, the carpenter, would advise him soon enough.

"Mr Keegan, pass word forward. My compliments to Mr Lovegrove, and he'll have to spare some of his men to clear the wreckage aft."

Gironde was still firing. The broadsides were arriving at regular intervals, although none caused the devastation of the first, and, as the ships drew apart, they became less and less effective.

"Cease firing!"

The two ships were so far apart now that it was not worth wasting shot, especially as there was so much to do on deck. Forward, the jib boom had been hauled aboard, the headsails taken down and stowed. Another party under Lovegrove's supervision was clearing with axes the wreckage of the mizzen topgallant on the quarterdeck. A few men had been killed—he could not stop to count or even ask—and had been dragged to the foot of the main mast, while the wounded were being carried below to the cockpit. Guns were being moved with handspikes and tackles, their barrels inspected by the gun captains before reloading, coigns were being adjusted. A party of waisters under a boatswain's mate was throwing more sand on deck and filling the fire buckets.

Soon!

Through his glass Penhaligon saw similar activity on *Gironde*, although he had no way of knowing how much damage she had suffered. *Avenger*'s carronades, which had not come into action until late in the affray, must have caused considerable damage on her maindeck, but it was below, on the gun deck, that *Avenger*'s guns had concentrated. Was it possible, he wondered, that more than one or two of those guns, or more than a handful of gunners, could still be in action? There was no doubt that *Gironde* had taken a terrible pounding. Despite the loss of the headsails and the mizzen topgallant, he still felt disposed to continue the action. *Gironde* must be on the verge of surrender.

"Bring her before the wind, Mr McNeil."

A cheer went up from the crew on deck as they realised that *Avenger* was going in to attack. The men kneeling by guns or crouching at braces, the waisters and topmen and powder boys were bright-eyed, anticipating victory. Rennie at the wheel was actually humming.

"Sir! You'd better come, sir! We're making water fast." It was Lambert, the carpenter, grey of face and short of breath, for he was not a young man and he had run up from below.

"What's the damage?"

"Four or five shots below the waterline, sir, one of them astern. Twenty-four pounders, I'd guess."

"Can't you plug them?"

"No, sir, begging your pardon, sir, them's too big."

"So, what's to be done?"

"They'll need a fother, sir. Even then—" He shook his head as though he could not bring himself to express his opinion.

"If we get the pumps working?"

"You'll need them, sir, in any case, if we're to stay afloat."

"Very well. Mr McNeil, go below, if you please, and see what can be done. Mr Lovegrove, get some men on the pumps, and quickly. Mr Lacey, detail another party to be at Mr Lambert's disposal."

He knew that Lambert would not exaggerate and, indeed, he would not have come aloft himself unless he was seriously concerned. Holing below the waterline was the fear of every captain, for, quite apart from the danger of sinking, a ship would become heavier and more unmanageable as she sank lower in the water until eventually, when she failed to respond, she became waterlogged and, as far as the enemy was concerned, a sitting target.

That had not happened yet.

"Steady as she goes. Mr Meldrum, report when your guns are ready."

181

Even if the carpenter's prognostications were correct and *Avenger* was slowly sinking, he had no intention of calling off the attack.

TWENTY

WITH her stern so low in the water that the helmsman had
to use both hands and the weight of his body to turn the
wheel, *Avenger* wallowed towards the shore. She was almost
waterlogged, but not quite. It was still touch and go whether
she would reach the beach.

"Cape Creus, sir," Lubbock had said, spreading the map
before his captain. "You see—Cabo, that means 'cape', sir.
If we come in under its lee we'll have shelter, and it's a sandy
shore."

"Very well, Mr Lubbock. Thank you."

It wasn't shelter he was worried about so much as finding
bottom. After twelve hours during which a dozen teams,
working in succession, had exhausted themselves at the pumps
and, despite the fothers which, as Lambert had predicted,
could only restrict but not stop the flow of water into the
hold, *Avenger* had got lower and lower in the water until she
was now scarcely manageable. But he could not, would not,
lose his ship so near to safety.

They were hardly more than a cable's length from shore
now. He saw a bay enclosed by a sandy beach on which there
were no signs of habitation, or indeed of vegetation apart
from a few stunted trees and some esparto grass. It was, he
imagined, a bleak, shadeless headland, too barren for farming
and too far from the nearest town of Figueras to encourage
habitation. So much the better.

He wondered how *Gironde* was faring. Obviously unaware
of *Avenger*'s plight, she had pulled away, licking her wounds,
and, with a wind on the quarter, had soon become no more

than a dot on the horizon. He wondered whether she would reach port.

"We are going to do it, sir," McNeil said, and, indeed, *Avenger* was now no more than a hundred yards from shore. But there were still problems, immense problems, as Penhaligon knew. With water still pouring into the hold despite the frantic pumping, he would have no time to sound bottom and, when he had taken some of the load from her decks, he would have to run her straight ashore.

"Let go the anchor! Lower away the longboat! Mr Love-grove, have a party ready at tackles."

They had been rigged on the maindeck, ready the moment *Avenger* hove-to to take the weight of eighteen-pounder guns, which must be swayed up and lowered with immense care and precision into the longboat. In the cutter, working parties would be ready to manhandle guns with rope and tackle once they were ashore. With *Avenger* beached, it was essential that they could still defend themselves.

"Steady on that tackle! Watch out below!"

The delicate, nerve-racking task of swaying out the guns was under way. Ashore, in the deepest part of the bay, another party was clearing the beach of rocks and erecting a rampart which would form some protection against attack from the landward side.

Penhaligon watched and occasionally barked an order, as under the lashing tongues of their petty officers the various parties went about their tasks. The ship was already lighter by four guns and, according to McNeil, was slightly higher in the water, but they would have to move another two guns at least before dark.

Shadows were lengthening, and the beach with the higher ground behind was already in gloom. Only the headlands which marked the entrance to the bay were in sunlight, and he could see the guns in position, the look-outs which Meldrum had posted, and the rough shelters they had raised against the night. Food and water were being ferried across in the gig, while the cutter, which had already made a dozen journeys, was going across again laden with shot.

"It's almost dark, sir," Carew observed. "Do you think that in these conditions—?"

"Mr Carew!" Penhaligon interrupted. "I am quite capable of judging the light. We need to take two more guns off her tonight, if we are to save her, and even then we shall continue pumping."

"Aye, aye, sir. I only meant—", but the captain was already out of hearing.

All night long the pumps clanked, and when dawn came *Avenger* was still afloat, although noticeably lower in the water. Penhaligon wondered how much more water she could take without sinking.

"Ready, Mr Lovegrove? Get those men working."

The admonition was unnecessary, for the men had been on deck and waiting for the last half-hour, since the first show of dawn had streaked the sky.

"Steady with those tackles! Ready? Lower away!"

All through the morning the work continued, and by noon *Avenger* was ready. The kedge anchor had been set, while ashore a hundred men stood at ropes and winches. *Avenger* emerged slowly from the sea.

It was uncomfortably hot. With the sun overhead and scarcely a breath of wind to freshen the air, the crew, stripped to the waist, sweated and swore as they toiled with cauldrons of steaming pitch across the burning sand to the upturned hull where the holes, already plugged by the carpenter, were being packed with oakum, while more of the crew were caulking seams and hammering the copper bottom. The jib boom, which had been shortened by a foot or two, had been reseated and lashed to the bowsprit, ready for headsails to be bent as soon as *Avenger* was seaworthy, while on the headlands and the rampart behind the beach the gunners and the defence party blessed their good fortune that, for once, they had been given the easy job.

"Sail ho!"

For a moment everyone stopped working, and the men with the caulking irons wondered whether those loafers on the headland would have to stir themselves after all.

But it was only a lugger, too far off to notice the upturned frigate. A few more hours of daylight, Penhaligon thought, and then the night : by dawn tomorrow they should be ready to get *Avenger* back into the water.

They kept to their target. When darkness fell and the exhausted crew threw themselves on the sand and, still grumbling, fell asleep, *Avenger*'s hull had been repaired, her jib boom was in position, the kedge anchor had been laid. Tomorrow the wearying process would be reversed, *Avenger* would be refloated, guns, stores and ammunition would be swayed aboard : by tomorrow noon at the latest *Avenger* would be ready for sea.

Resting with his back against a tree, Penhaligon looked out across the bay and, feeling a wind on his cheek, the first wind of the day, he knew that luck still ran for him. Despite crippling damage, *Avenger* had out-fought and out-manoeuvred *Gironde*; the French ship, unaware of her advantage, had withdrawn. Next time they met, *Avenger* would finish the job.

He thought of Maddalena, Duchess of Potenza, of Emma Hamilton, of the Marquesa de Cullera y Alicante and other women he had known. And he thought of Clarissa, with her boyish figure, her pert, lively face and her sense of fun. He knew, or rather repeated to himself what he had known for a long time, that she was the only one for him. For the first time he found himself wishing that a voyage was over and looking forward to the day they arrived in port. Clarissa!

"Sir." It was McNeil, who had come to join him in the darkness. "I hope I'm not disturbing you."

"No. Sit down. I was just thinking how much we still have to do."

"I was thinking the opposite, sir—how much we have done."

"You're right. They have all worked well. Tomorrow, when we get to sea, I'll tell them so."

"Do you think, sir, that an issue of rum would be appropriate?"

"Why not? Let them enjoy it while they can, for they'll be fighting again soon."

McNeil lowered himself carefully into the sand and rested his back against a tree. "You intend to go on?"

"Of course. That's what we came for, to get *Gironde*. That's what I intend to do."

"Yes, sir, but with respect she'll be in Barcelona by now. She can hole up there as she did before."

"I know. That's what I have been considering." He paused for a moment and then asked, "Have you been to Barcelona?"

"No, sir."

"I have, once—on *Prince George*, before the war."

"Can you remember what it was like?"

"Not as well as I would wish."

"Sir?"

"It occurs to me, Mr McNeil, that if *Gironde* won't come out to fight, we may have to go in and get her."

TWENTY-ONE

THERE was still an hour to dawn as *Avenger* reached the approaches of Barcelona. It was a warm night, overcast but with sufficient breeze to fill the headsails, and on the decks, which had been cleared for action, the crew watched and waited without talking, for they had been enjoined to silence, and wondered how long it would be before the shore batteries opened up.

In fact, there was no sign of activity ashore. There was no moon, and it could well be that the sentries in the fort on the headland they had just passed had mistaken them for a merchantman or a fishing vessel. One boat, a ketch, just weighing anchor had hailed them but had apparently accepted Penhaligon's grunted reply. Towards the shore on either side small trading ships and fishing boats were tied up, but here in mid-stream the passage was clear.

How much farther? Relying on memory, for the charts only showed the docks with their warehouses and berths, Penhaligon tried to form a mental picture of the shipyard. Like Deptford and Greenwich, it was seaward of the commercial port; he remembered a ship of the line they were building there—could it have been *El Cid*?—and the runways which were bigger and better equipped than any he had seen in England.

He looked at his watch: five-twelve, another ten, fifteen minutes to first light. Astern the sky was clearing, although reluctantly, as though the storm which had followed them all yesterday was still threatening.

"*Ah del barco*!" That was another hail from shore.

He could see nothing except the outlines of ships and what looked like warehouses and, further inland, a few lights on the hill.

It wouldn't be long now. *Gironde*, he thought, where are you?

It was possible, of course, that she was not at Barcelona at all, that after the battle she had sailed north to Marseilles or Toulon, in which case *Avenger's* desperate gamble would be in vain.

"There, sir—ahead!" It was McNeil who saw her.

She rode at anchor a hundred yards from shore, with her yards lowered and only the guns of her larboard side run out. There was a mass of spars and canvas and cordage on deck as though the shipwrights, after making their preparations, had decided to postpone their work for another day. Apart from the larboard guns and the sentry who, to his credit, shouted a warning before *Avenger* had fully emerged from the mist, she seemed to be in an even worse state of preparedness than when *Avenger* had come out of the darkness two dawns ago.

"Stand by the starboard guns, Mr Meldrum. Fire as you bear!"

To the roll of a drum *Gironde's* crew, or such of them as were still aboard, came tumbling out. Once again as *Avenger* approached, Penhaligon saw utter confusion. There was only one officer on the quarterdeck, although another, still dressed in his undergarments, was just appearing. There were shouts and orders and counter-orders: one man waited forlornly by the capstan, ready to weigh anchor.

"Fire!"

Avenger's broadside, at point-blank range, rocked *Gironde* to her keelson. Only one of her guns was even manned, although other crews were mustering, breech covers were being torn off, gun captains were adjusting coigns and shouting for powder and shot.

"Fire!"

The second broadside made much of their work unnecessary, for three of *Gironde*'s larboard guns were hit and a dozen men lay dead or wounded on deck.

"Prepare to go about!"

As *Avenger* turned, a gun from the shore opened up, the muzzle flash clearly visible in the half-light, but whether the gunners were equally unprepared or were perhaps afraid of hitting the wrong ship, the shot landed upstream, to the alarm and consternation of other vessels berthed at the quay.

"Fire as you bear, Mr Meldrum!"

"Cock your locks! Take aim! Fire!"

The broadside from the larboard guns was the most devastating of all. Aimed at *Gironde*'s gun deck, which had taken such a terrible pounding two dawns ago, it smashed through the hull and gun ports, killing many of the crew, started fires below deck which the bewildered and terrified waisters and loblolly boys were unable to control, and, with half the officers, including the captain, ashore, finally broke *Gironde*'s resistance.

"Fire!" Avenger's guns were at it again.

"Main braces! Back the main topsail!"

There was only one thing to do now. Despite the guns on the hill—and to starboard, no doubt, although he had heard nothing from that side yet—*Avenger* must stay to finish the job. With dawn fully breaking, although low clouds limited vision, there would be no chance to turn again. His plan, which had succeeded so far beyond his wildest expectations, was surprise, a quick strike and away. He remembered that they still had to pass the batteries downstream.

"Fire!"

It was difficult to see beyond the mainmast for smoke from the guns. Swab out with mops to extinguish any smouldering remains of powder, reload, gun tackles forward, a quick aim over the barrel by the gun captain, a raised arm to signal readiness, then, on the order, "Fire!"

Broadside followed broadside as *Gironde*, defenceless now, for even the officers on the poop had gone, reeled before the weight of metal and, as gaping holes appeared near the water-line, began to list.

"Keep it up, lads!" That was Meldrum, shaken for once from his usual phlegm.

There was musket fire from ashore, Penhaligon realised; he heard the whistle of shot, and young Keegan, who a moment ago had been jumping with excitement, was suddenly sitting by the taffrail, white faced, nursing his leg.

"She's afire!"

For a moment, as though by common impulse, the deck went quiet, *Avenger*'s guns stopped firing, and then, from all along the ship, came a mighty cheer.

"Well done, lads!" Penhaligon shouted, as soon as he could make himself heard. "One more broadside, Mr Meldrum, then we'll be on our way."

As *Avenger* moved downstream the flames were already consuming *Gironde*. From the gun deck they leapt upwards, greedily devouring hull, bulwarks and maindeck, and were licking round the forward mast. The heat, even at a hundred yards' distance, was intense, too hot for comfort, Penhaligon thought, as he shouted, anxious for his own ship, "Mr Lovegrove, have those fire buckets ready!"

The flames presented another danger, for the light, which was still poor, was suddenly brightened by the glare from *Gironde*.

A salvo from the shore guns straddled *Avenger*, smashing through the maindeck and killing two at number four gun. The soldiers were still firing: he could see them now, on the left bank, standing with feet astride, leaning forward as they aimed. The batteries downstream would be waiting.

The wind had dropped! He realised it at once as *Avenger*, responding sluggishly to the helm, moved slowly towards the sea.

Another battery had opened up now, and a small ship, an armed brig, was challenging.

"Fire as you bear, Mr Meldrum, Gun captains to find their own targets."

There were too many hostile forces against them to concentrate on any one. Having completed her mission, *Avenger* could only accept what punishment the enemy could inflict.

"It's raining, sir." That was Hardcastle.

So it was, by God! A few heavy spots were followed in a moment by a steady downpour. It was, he realised, the most fortunate stroke of all. The rain, which came driving over the beam and soaked everyone on deck within minutes, would be their ally. Although it was heavy enough to hamper *Avenger*'s guns, it would hamper equally the guns on shore. No crew liked to work in these conditions when cartridges had to be sheltered under canvas until the moment of opening the breech, when carriages slipped and slithered about the deck, when handspikes failed to grip, and the feet of men at tackles slid from under them.

Even more important at this moment was the light. A heavy raincloud had brought a return of semi-darkness, so that the gunners on the hill, cursing as they sheltered their charges from the rain, would soon be even more hampered as they looked over open sights.

"Steady as she goes!"

The wind was fair, despite the cloud, and *Avenger*'s sails, soaked more effectively than Lovegrove's bucket parties had ever managed, retained every breath of it.

"There's the headland, sir," McNeil called, "over to starboard."

The last obstacle, if one could forget the brig which was still following, popping away with her six-pounders, like a small dog yapping on the heels of a mastiff.

"There she goes!"

They saw the gunflashes and in a moment, before they heard the reports, saw the spurts of water astern.

"They are firing blind, sir," McNeil said. "They'll never hit us."

"Unless they are lucky."

"No, sir." McNeil smiled. "With respect, sir, all the luck seems to be on our side."

Penhaligon nodded. It was true. As Nelson had told him at that never-to-be-forgotten meeting at the Capodimonte Palace, "A commander needs skill, judgment, but, above all, luck. In my experience, boldness brings its own luck."

The guns of the shore battery had stopped firing now, perhaps because their captains could see nothing to fire at. The brig, too, had called off the chase and was creeping back, tail between her legs, to her berth.

Upstream, the sky was red with the funeral pyre of *Gironde*.

TWENTY-TWO

It was a fine day in early summer when *Avenger* sailed into Mahon. The town and the sleeping hills were bathed in sunshine, the sea was calm and there was a scent of mimosa in the air. As they entered the harbour Penhaligon saw that the five merchantmen they had captured had all gone, presumably sold and now being used by local traders or fishermen, but *El Cid* remained. Riding at anchor in a little-used corner of the harbour, she looked like an elderly spinster at a ball, proud but unwanted.

Jamie was at the quayside.

"What happened? Did you find *Gironde*?"

"Yes." Penhaligon looked round distractedly, seeking Clarissa.

"Well? Did you engage her?"

"What? Oh, yes. We fought her."

"And?"

"She was destroyed."

"Cocky!" Jamie seized his hand as they crossed the square. "This is splendid news. Father—everyone—will be delighted. Does Naples know, and Gibraltar?"

"Not yet. I must leave tomorrow, as soon as we've taken on water. Admiral Nelson must know."

"Of course." Impulsively, Jamie took his friend's arm and assisted him into the carriage.

"Where is Clarissa?"

Jamie did not reply, in fact he appeared to be so busy giving orders to the coachman that they were in the centre of town, distracted by the stalls and taverns and slow-moving traffic, before Penhaligon asked again, "Where is Clarissa?"

"She's away. She went to some friends on the other side of the island."

"When did she leave?"

"This morning."

"How long will she be away?"

"Three, four days. I don't know."

Penhaligon felt joy draining away so that he was scarcely conscious of the sunshine or the crowds or the fountains wreathed by miniature rainbows or the comforting clip-clop of the horse's hooves.

"What's happened, Jamie? Why isn't she here?"

Greatly embarrassed, Jamie took a letter from his pocket and handed it to his friend.

"Cocky darling," it read. "If I didn't love you so much I should say, 'How could you?'

"I was awake on the night you left, awake because I couldn't bear the thought of losing you. I heard you knock at Isabelita's door, I heard you leave an hour later. I hope you enjoyed her company!

"Don't laugh at me, Cocky, when I say that my heart was broken. To think of you with that woman—and only an hour or less after you had told me that you loved me and that there would never be anyone else.

"You are what you are, Cocky, and there's no altering that. I shall leave as soon as I see *Avenger* entering the bay, and I must ask you not to follow.

"Goodbye, Cocky. It is better this way, although at the moment I can't anticipate with anything but distress the long years without you.

Your Clarissa."

He screwed the letter in his hand and thrust it into his pocket. "Damn!" He turned to Jamie and demanded, fiercely, "Did you know? Did she tell you what she had written?"

195

"Not exactly." Jamie looked miserable. "I suppose I guessed."

"Then the sooner I tell my story the better. You know, Jamie, that I've never been exactly an angel, but I do love Clarissa. I want to marry her, and since she's not here and I must sail tomorrow I can only appeal to you for help."

When they entered the house they found that Sir Hubert, who was never at his best at this time of day, was still in bed, and the two friends retired to the drawing-room where, an aeon ago it seemed, they had laughed and played indifferent whist and been happy. Through the open windows they could see the garden, with azaleas, oleanders and a flaming mass of bougainvillea in blossom, the town, with wood smoke drifting lazily over rooftops, and, beyond, the maquis-covered slopes that edged the sea.

"I did go to the marquesa's room that evening," Penhaligon explained, "but for a reason." He hesitated. "I'm sorry to tell you this, Jamie, but your marquesa is a fraud."

"Isabelita! But that's not possible. She's done so much for me, for England, and at great danger to herself."

"What has she done?"

"Well, you know. She's taken me in, hidden me when necessary, whenever I've set foot in Spain. She's passed information, valuable information of ship movements."

"She didn't tell you what she told me, that she had seen *Gironde* heading south."

"She was mistaken, as she sometimes is. After all, she's not a sailor. Her information isn't always correct."

"I can imagine! You remember that I asked her about look-outs: just herself, she said, and an old nurse of eighty-four."

"That's right. There is an old nurse. I've seen her. Don't you understand, Cocky, that's as much as she dared risk? She has been—she still is—in constant danger."

"She's a brave woman, all right. I'll give you that."

"And the risks she has taken have been for us."

"No. I'm sorry, Jamie, but you are wrong. Oh, she's a spy all right, a spy for the French."

"I don't believe it!"

"I guessed at once, at the luncheon table, when she told her so convincing story."

"Well, if it's true."

"It's not. Unfortunately she chose the wrong person to tell it to. I knew that her story about her English grandmother and her sister who died on the guillotine was nonsense."

"How?"

"Well, I know little enough about the aristocracy, but my uncle, who is also my guardian, told me once in a moment of weakness that as a young man he had been disappointed in love: that was why he had never married, although if you want my private opinion I'd say that his figure—he weighs twenty stone—and his temperament had something to do with it. But one thing I do remember—the young lady who turned him down eventually married someone else. She became Lady Winchester."

"So? She could be a younger generation, Isabelita's aunt."

"I doubt it. The Lady Winchester my uncle was in love with is still alive: she is, I believe, in her nineties."

Jamie was clearly perplexed. "That's strange, if what you say is true: but, knowing you, it's quite possible that you've got the name wrong."

"No, I'm quite sure." Penhaligon leant forward in his chair. "It was all too convenient, Jamie. When Baghot and I went ashore she was there, all alone in her summer house, almost waiting to be captured. And it occurred to me afterwards that *Avenger* could hardly have come into the lee of the headland unnoticed. Someone must have seen her. The marquesa knew who we were, she knew the name of our ship: I realised then that she wanted to be captured."

"But why?"

"To be taken to Minorca—knowing she would have a safe return. Perhaps the French were dissatisfied with the information they were getting from their agent in Mahon, although some of it must have been useful, for when we challenged *Lyon* a week or two back Lacoste, her captain, knew the British code. At any rate, for whatever reason, the marquesa decided to come and see for herself."

"And that's why you went to her room?"

"Yes, and that was the only reason," Penhaligon said. "You must explain this to Clarissa, Jamie, for it's the truth."

"I'll do my best." Jamie smiled. "And I'll tell you one thing : whatever she said in that letter, she loves you."

Penhaligon looked doubtful. "I hope you're right." Then, "I went to the marquesa's room because I had to find *Gironde*. I didn't believe her story about seeing her heading south. In the first place, I doubted whether *Gironde* could have been ready for sea so soon; in the second place, if she had been at sea she wouldn't have taken that course for Gibraltar."

"Of course not! To clear Cap Nao she would have passed Cullera well out of sight of land."

"That's what I thought."

"So, what did you do? Did you question her?"

"No, quite the opposite. I wanted her to question me, which she did eventually, although it took some time."

"What did you tell her?"

"I told her, since she asked, that after taking her to Cullera *Avenger* would continue south. I said we would be looking for *Gironde* in the approaches to Gibraltar."

"Although, in fact, you intended to sail north?"

"Yes. I waited on tenterhooks for a time before I could be sure that she was going to pass on the information. After that, I knew where we should find *Gironde*."

Jamie looked glum. "It seems that I made a fool of myself. I've never doubted that she was genuine."

"It wasn't your fault," Penhaligon said. "She is a beautiful woman, and clever. To maintain her deception she had to pass you some information that was genuine."

"Small consolation!" Jamie sat back in his chair, crest-fallen and perhaps wondering how this would affect his career. Despite the excitement and danger of the last few months, he still yearned for the sea. "You said she passed on the false information you gave her, but how?"

"Through her agent in Mahon. After I left her room I heard her go downstairs quietly. Shortly afterwards I saw him crossing the lawn."

"Who?"

Penhaligon's expression hardened. "I think, Jamie, you only have to open that door."

Jamie had crossed the room in a few strides and as he flung open the door he was in time to see a figure in the hall.

"Thomas! Stop!"

"Don't worry," Penhaligon said. "He won't get far."

Even as he said it they heard a crash and the sound of a blow, and, almost directly, Baghot appeared carrying the inert form of the butler. "Ran into me, sir, accidental like. Should have looked where he was going."

"So it was Thomas after all."

"I'm afraid so. He'd been passing information for some time, I'd guess."

"But how?"

"Through Heldstrom, the Swede. You'll never touch him, I'm afraid, even if you could prove it, but he's the one who has been running messages to and from Spain; to Paris, too, I dare say. A pity he's a neutral."

It was dawn the following morning when Penhaligon drove down the hill towards the sea. It was cool, pleasantly cool before the heat of the day, and the labourers setting off for the fields with their mattocks and hoes and the housewives going to meet the fishing fleet were bare-headed and bare-armed and, despite the early hour, bade him a cheerful good morning. Baghot was waiting for him on the quay.

"Give my respects to your master," Penhaligon said to the

coachman, "and to Mr Jamie. I'm sorry Mr Jamie was still asleep when I left. Tell him I'll see him soon."

"Aye, sir. I'll do that."

Heldstrom was in harbour again, he saw, and there appeared to be unusual activity on deck. The local police were aboard, and across the still water came the sound of argument. One day, he thought, I'll sink *Heldstrom*; neutral or not, I'll sink her.

"Coffee, sir, burgoo?" In his cabin Baghot had already prepared the usual unpalatable breakfast.

"Thank you, although I'm not hungry." Penhaligon looked out of the open port. "What's happening on *Heldstrom*?"

"An accident, sir, or so I'm told."

"What sort of accident?"

"Heldstrom, sir, the captain; he's dead."

"Good God!" Looking across the dazzling expanse of water, he saw the police, apparently satisfied, returning to shore. "How did it happen?"

"Don't know, sir, not for sure. Heard he had a fall."

"On his ship?"

"No, sir. Last night, I'm told, he felt the urge, as they say —went to one of the houses of ill-repute."

"And?"

"Well, sir, I'm not sure exactly, but apparently he'd just said goodbye to the lady and was walking out by the back stairs—to avoid gossip, sir, if you get me meaning—when he fell—thirty, forty feet, so I'm told, into the yard."

"And was killed?"

"Broke his neck, sir, clean as a whistle. Just proves what the good book says, sir: the wages of sin—"

"Baghot!" Penhaligon said. "What do you know about this? You were out last evening, in one of the houses of ill-repute, I shouldn't wonder. Did you kill him?"

"Me, sir? No, sir. I don't have to go to those sort of places when I feel the urge. There's a young lady in town—well, two, as a matter of fact—"

"Did you kill him?"

"No, sir. Like I said, sir : I think it was an accident."

Avenger cleared the headland within the hour and, to catch the wind, clawed her way northwards towards Cavaleria, where, with the wind on her beam, she could make directly for Sardinia. She would be in Naples in three days.

"Well, sir," McNeil said, "the admiral should be pleased. We've done all that he asked."

"Yes, he'll be glad to know that *Gironde* has gone. I wonder what he will find for us next."

It was exhilarating to stand on the quarterdeck with the sun on your back, the spray flying and a fresh wind in your face. Ahead the sea was blue, and the sky, meeting on the horizon, was even bluer. A few gulls, wheeling over the stern, pitched their cries against the thrum of wind in the shrouds, while from below, in the orlop, came the monotonous clanking of pumps.

"It's a pleasant enough island," McNeil observed, feeling, correctly, that his captain was in the mood to talk. "I wonder when we'll call here again."

Yes, Penhaligon thought; I wonder. Anything could happen. With the British chasing across the world, to West Indies, the Atlantic, the Mediterranean, the Channel, even to India, in pursuit of the reluctant French, it might be months, even years, before he saw Clarissa again.

"Sir! Do you see—there on the cliffs? Two people, friends of yours, perhaps."

"Give me your glass." He took it eagerly and focused on the sunlit island. Yes : his heart gave a lurch. Two people, how could he ever mistake them? Clarissa and Jamie.

He cleared his throat. "Two points to larboard, if you please. There's something I've forgotten."

As they approached the shore he could see Clarissa quite clearly, her hair and her skirt blowing in the wind, her hand shading her eyes.

"Take her in as close as she'll go. Then heave-to. Mr

Lovegrove, get ready to lower away my gig."

When *Avenger*, with main topsail backed, glided to within a cable's length of shore, Clarissa and Jamie had disappeared, but he saw that there was a ravine with a stream running through it leading to the beach.

"I'm going ashore, Mr McNeil. I won't be long."

"Aye, aye, sir." McNeil accompanied him to the companion and said, in a low voice, "Good luck!"

She was there under the olive trees which grew to the margin of the beach. She stood quite still, not waving or even smiling, and he thought: 'She must understand. I'd give anything—anything, to make her understand.'

"Here we are, sir. Don't get your feet wet."

As the gig ran on to the sand he left Baghot and walked with measured step towards the trees. His heart was beating strongly, and he thought: 'Please! If I never have luck any more, let her understand.'

She was still standing there, hands clasped before her, unsmiling.

"Clarissa!" Without altering his stride, he called her name, and at once, as though this, the timbre of his voice, was all she needed, she came to life. A grin, the delightful, urchin grin he loved, split her face, and she ran towards him, hair streaming, and threw herself into his arms.

"Cocky! Cocky, darling!"

"Clarissa!" He held her so tightly that in a moment she had to plead for breath. "I thought I'd lost you. Only minutes ago I was wondering whether I would ever see you again. I love you, Clarissa. I've said it often enough, but it's true. I love you."

"And I love you, Cocky. I always shall."

"Well?" Jamie, after a decent interval, had emerged from the trees. "Sorry I couldn't see you off this morning, but, as you see, I had other things to do."

Penhaligon smiled. "Thanks, Jamie. When we are married we'll call our first son after you."

"When will that be, I wonder. It looks like being a long war."

"I can't wait so long," Penhaligon said.

"Nor I," said Clarissa.

"Very well." He made up his mind on the instant and knew that this was what he wanted to do. "Come with me now, Clarissa."

"All right." His heart went out to her as, without thought of clothes, money or family complications, she agreed. She looked up at him with her perky smile. "I've always wanted to see Naples."

"Jamie?" Penhaligon looked at his friend.

"All right," Jamie said. "I'll explain it to Father. I don't doubt he'll have a fit."

"Tell him I'm marrying a hero," Clarissa said, "someone he'll be proud of. Tell him I'm marrying the English Captain."

The gig pulled from the shore and was soon all but lost on the sun-reflecting water: then it was clear again, silhouetted against the dark hull of *Avenger*. He watched his sister lean on her lover's arm and, with one foot on the gunwale, step across to the ladder.

What happened then was not clear, they were too far away, but he saw Penhaligon catch her, pull her from the water and lift her bodily on to the ladder. Although she was so far away, he could see, or perhaps imagined that he could see, her face split by a grin, and he heard—of this he was quite sure—the sound of laughter.